Secrets...hopes...dreams...

Welcome to

Silver Spires

where
School Friends
are
forever!

Collect the *School Friends* series:

Welcome to Silver Spires
Drama at Silver Spires
Rivalry at Silver Spires
Princess at Silver Spires
Secrets at Silver Spires
Star of Silver Spires

Welcome to
Silver Spires

Ann Bryant

USBORNE

For Lesley Hodgson, my best friend,
and dorm mom par excellence!

My grateful thanks to Cally Fosbery and
Emma Stone for all their help

First published in the UK in 2008 by Usborne Publishing Ltd.,
Usborne House, 83-85 Saffron Hill, London EC1N 8RT, England.
www.usborne.com

Series cover design by Sally Griffin
Cover illustration by Suzanne Sales/New Division

The name Usborne and the devices ♀ 🎈 are Trade Marks of
Usborne Publishing Ltd.

This is a work of fiction. The characters, incidents, and dialogues are
products of the author's imagination and are not to be construed as real. Any
resemblance to actual events or persons, living or dead, is entirely coincidental.

A CIP catalogue record for this book is available from the British Library.

First published in America in 2012 AE.
PB ISBN 9780794531461   ALB ISBN 9781601302694
JF AMJJASOND/12   01575/1
Printed in Dongguan, Guangdong, China.

Chapter One

"Not long now, Katy," said Dad, taking his eyes off the road for a second to glance sideways at me.

A shiver of excitement mixed up with big-time nervousness ran through me and I turned around to check on Buddy, my pet rabbit, who was lying in his basket in the back seat. He blinked his velvety eyes at me, just like he had done every other time I'd checked on him during this three-hour-long car journey.

"Almost there, Bud! Just think, you're about to make lots of new friends!"

Dad laughed. "I think he'd be saying exactly the same thing to you, if he could talk, Kates!"

And that sent another of those shivers rushing through me because I was about to start a brand-new life and it suddenly seemed totally scary. I'd read plenty of books about kids at boarding schools, but I had no idea what it would actually feel like to be at one myself, with a dorm mom instead of a mom and a dad, sleeping in a dormitory with five other girls that I'd never met before, and walking to classes every morning in less than a minute.

For the last few days I'd done nothing but pack and unpack and repack my suitcases because I'd changed my mind so often about what clothes to take. Even now I wasn't sure that I'd brought the right amount. "What if I've got too much stuff, Dad?"

"Then you can just leave some of it in your trunk."

"But what if I've not packed *enough*?"

Dad laughed. "Then you can bring more stuff at fall break. Stop worrying, Kates!"

"I don't want you to come up to the dorm, Dad."

"That's fine."

"But what if you leave and then I wish you *had* come up to the dorm after all? I'll be really sad."

"So maybe it would be best if I *did* come up to the dorm then."

"No because then I'll definitely be sad when you've gone."

Dad laughed and patted my leg. "It'll all be fine. Remember what Mom said. It's only fear of the unknown that makes us worry. Half an hour after I've gone you'll be right as rain."

I wasn't so sure about that. And although I didn't say anything else out loud, the questions kept going on inside my head. *What if I don't like the other girls in my dorm? What if they don't like me? What if I can't find my way around?*

There was only one thing that would calm me down and that was sketching, so I pulled my pad and pencil out of my backpack and before I knew it I'd covered a double page with designs for dresses and boots. They weren't new designs though because I couldn't concentrate on being creative when my mind was on school, wondering how long it would take me to get used to having all my meals in an enormous cafeteria and doing my homework with lots of other people in the same room instead of by myself, often in front of the TV. That thought made me suddenly feel homesick, which was a bad sign as I hadn't even arrived at school yet.

7

I knew I was really going to miss Mom and Dad. Especially Mom. I don't have any brothers or sisters so Mom and I are very close, but now I'm on my way to boarding school, Los Angeles seems even further away than it did when Mom first went over there and it was just me and Dad living at home. At least Mom and I will be able to call and e-mail each other, but I won't see her again until Christmas.

It was less than a year ago when Mom and Dad first brought up the idea of boarding school, and I remember how I was instantly filled with excitement at the thought of every single day being like a sleepover. Mom had laughed and put her hands up like a policeman. "Whoa there! It's not decided yet, Kates! Dad and I are just thinking you might be happier in a boarding school than being at home now I know I'm going to be away filming more and more."

Everything had happened so fast. One minute Mom was an actress who nobody had really heard of, and the next minute she'd gotten the part of Lee Brook in a sitcom that just about everyone in the world watches – *The Fast Lane*. It was only a small part at first, but then it gradually got bigger because the director and lots of other important people loved the way Mom acted it. In the end they wanted

Mom's character to become one of the main parts in the new series, but it meant Mom would have to live in L.A., and that's when she'd started to think I might be happier in a boarding school.

So here I am, on my way to a new life, remembering how Mom hugged me tight before she went off to California two days ago, and said, "We'll be together for all of the main holidays, Kates!" But right now the Christmas holidays seem an eternity away.

Dad threw me another glance. "What's that you're sketching?"

"Nothing much." I snapped the book shut and sat up straighter than straight.

"Oh! I get it! Something I'm not supposed to see." He pretended to be upset.

"Course not!" I laughed. "It's just that I'm going to watch where we're going from now on."

I was quiet after that, staring out of the window at the houses and shops flashing by, then the trees and fields as we went further out into the country. It's weird having a mom who's so famous. When she first appeared in *The Fast Lane*, I thought it was the coolest thing ever, especially when some of the kids at school wanted my autograph, as though having a famous mom made me famous too. And they kept asking me if Mom knew other famous people, and I liked the feeling I got when they all gasped and said, "Wow! That's so cool!" And some of the younger ones at school would point me out to their moms in loud voices on the playground. "Look, that girl's mom is on TV! She's Lee Brook!" And suddenly everyone wanted to be my friend so I got loads of invitations to people's houses, and even the teachers used to tell me when they'd watched *The Fast Lane* the night before.

It was great getting all this attention, just like suddenly being allowed as much chocolate as I wanted, until one day the chocolate made me feel sick. You see, that's when I realized the attention had nothing at all to do with me. The kids at school only invited me to their houses because they wanted to get an invite back to my place so they could see Mom. And it grew really annoying when people asked me if Mom could get other famous people's autographs for them. In fact I started to wonder whether I had any *real* friends at all, and that was a great big scary thought, which made me wish I could switch the clocks back and just have an ordinary mom.

So then I talked to Mom and Dad about it lots, and Dad was always joking around, saying that he knew how I felt because it was the same for him at work – everyone being extra nice to him, just because he had a famous wife. Mom said she thought it would settle down when people got used to it, and then everything would be back to normal. She was wrong, though. It never went back to normal and I was never ever sure whether people liked me for myself, or just because I had a famous mom. There wasn't anything I could do to change things back to how they were before, but at least I could try my best not to make the same mistake again.

From the moment I knew I was going to boarding school miles away from home, I realized I had the chance for a brand-new start, so I made a great big decision. My plan is to keep Mom and her job a secret from everyone. Well, *nearly* everyone. The Head of the whole school, Ms. Carmichael, knows who my mother is, and so does Miss Carol, the dorm mom of Hazeldean, the boarding house that I'll be in. But they're both keeping the information totally confidential. So from now on I can be really sure that no one will know about Mom. That means I'll be able to tell for certain who my *real* friends are.

A feeling of determination went zapping through me just as we rounded a bend in the road and came across an arch of overhanging trees. I sat up straight and spoke in a gabble. "I remember this stretch of road from when I came on my orientation day. It reminded me of a tunnel. We're nearly there, aren't we, Dad?"

"Just around the corner if my memory serves me right," said Dad.

The next minute we came across the big blue sign with silver lettering...

Silver Spires Boarding School
For Girls Ages 11–18

"This is it!" I squeaked, as Dad turned into the long drive and I tried to catch my first glimpse of the Silver Spires main building.

A few seconds later the lane curved around to the right and there it stood, solid and grand in the distance, with its sweeping arches and dark old walls, its diamond shaped windowpanes and enormous front door, and best of all its tall spires that glinted and gleamed like silver in the sun. The sight of the building drowned my nervousness in the most magicky feeling of excitement that I was about to become part of a new and awesome, buzzing world. But a few seconds later the nervousness sprang back as we began to pass dorms with cars parked outside and girls and parents and dorm parents milling around, and occasionally a man in overalls carrying suitcases.

And before I knew it the road had forked off to the left and there was Hazeldean.

"Looks like we've come at a good time!" said Dad. "Not many cars here. I guess we've missed the rush."

I looked at my watch. Twenty-five to five. In the letter it said you could arrive at any time between three and five, so we must be among the last people. I undid my seat belt, feeling suddenly relieved that I'd decided to wear my jeans because most of the girls I could see were in either jeans or tracksuit pants. I'd so nearly worn my swirly layered skirt, and my new brown boots, and the beautiful blue dangly earrings, because those are the kinds of things I love wearing. But I absolutely did not want to stand out, especially not on my first day. All the same, my top half wasn't exactly plain because I was wearing one of Mom's tops. It shrunk in the wash, so it's too small for her but it fits me perfectly. It's made of what I call crinkly silk with a lacy part around the top and the cuffs, and it's brown but it looks as though it's faded in the sun. Mom says it looks great with my dark skin and hair. I think she might be a little biased though and I was beginning to wish I'd just worn a plain T-shirt.

"Hello, it's Katy, isn't it?" I'd just opened the car door and there was Miss Carol, the dorm mom, giving me a big smile. "Nice to see you again!" she said. I remembered her clearly from my last visit and really liked the way she made you feel so welcome. She shook hands with Dad. "Hello, Mr. Parsons. You've arrived at a good time. It's all been a little crazy, but it's quietened down again now." Then she spotted Buddy in the back. "Aha! A customer for Pets' Place. I'll find someone to show you where to take him." She chuckled. "Or is it her?"

"It's him," I answered, as a man with a luggage carrier appeared by the car.

"Good timing, Tony! This is Katy Parsons. I think she's in Amethyst dorm."

The man nodded at me then put my suitcases on the luggage carrier. "I'll check on the noticeboard, Miss C."

"You're welcome to go up to the dorm, Mr. Parsons," Miss Carol said to Dad. "Lots of parents have been settling their daughters in, though most of them have gone now."

Dad looked at me and I shook my head, the decision suddenly made. "It's okay, I'll go up on my own, actually."

Miss Carol nodded. "That's fine. Let's introduce you to one or two of the other sixth graders." She steered me away from Dad and toward the entrance to Hazeldean. "There's Mia Roberts. Perfect! Mia was one of the first to get here and she's in the same dorm as you, Katy, so she can take you up after you've registered."

The girl standing by the door was smaller than me, with a pale serious face and long blonde hair in a ponytail. She looked nice but I still felt a little anxious because everything was moving so fast and what if I didn't get the chance to say bye to Dad? Miss Carol must have realized. "Don't worry, Katy, you'll see your dad before he goes." She patted my shoulder, and I thought again how kind she was. Then she introduced me to Mia who broke into a big smile.

"Hi, Katy! You're in Amethyst dorm with me." She turned a little pink. "There are only two other girls from our dorm here so far – Jessica and Grace... except I seem to have lost them."

I nearly laughed because it sounded so funny, as though Mia thought it was *her* fault that the girls had gone missing. Miss Carol must have been thinking the same thing. "I'm sure they'll turn up!" she chuckled. Then more cars pulled up and off she rushed to greet them, talking over her shoulder. "I'll tell your dad you're just registering, Katy."

I nodded and saw that Dad was talking to another lady who I thought I recognized from my visit last time.

"That's Miss Fosbrook," said Mia, following my gaze. "She's the assistant dorm mom."

The hall at Hazeldean was filled with voices and laughter. It was obvious who were the older students because they were hugging each other and talking loud and fast, sharing their vacation news with shining eyes, and leaning forward to whisper their secrets.

"It feels funny being new, doesn't it?" said Mia, quietly to me.

I nodded. "I wish I could press a fast-forward button and know everyone, and be used to all the rules and everything."

Mia giggled. "Me too." Then she led me over to a noticeboard and pointed at the list with the heading *Amethyst*. "Look, these are the girls in our dorm."

We read the names out loud together. "Mia, Grace, Katy, Jessica, Naomi, Georgie."

Then Mia giggled again. "I remember Georgie from when I visited the school last year. She was totally nuts and didn't seem worried about anything.

She told me she was growing her hair and that next time we saw each other it'd be long enough for a ponytail. But she probably won't even remember me," Mia added in a slightly sorrowful voice.

I was just about to say that I was sure Georgie would remember her right away when a great boom came from across the hall. "Have you two girls registered?"

I turned around to see a stern-looking lady sitting at a table on the other side of the hall. She was peering at us over a pair of glasses with no rims.

"Miss Jennings, the dorm supervisor," whispered Mia out of the corner of her mouth. "I registered earlier. Come on." She hurried over to the table and I followed her.

Miss Jennings hardly glanced at me. "Join the line while it's nice and short," she said, then continued registering the girls in front of me.

"Scary!" mouthed Mia, rolling her eyes.

"You're not kidding!" I whispered.

At the back of the line we started talking in our normal voices. "Do you have a pet?" Mia asked.

"Yes, a rabbit…named Buddy."

"That's a cool name. I've got two guinea pigs, Porgy and Bess. I'll take you down to Pets' Place when your mom and dad have gone."

"Oh...I just came with my dad actually... Mom's away."

Something tightened inside me because this was the first time Mom had been mentioned.

"Hope your dad doesn't drive off with Buddy by mistake. That's what my parents did. We said our goodbyes really quickly so we wouldn't be too sad, only then they realized they'd driven off with Porgy and Bess so they had to come back and go through it all again!"

"Oh, poor you."

"Your turn next," she added.

At first I thought she meant that it was my turn to be sad, but then I saw that she was talking about the line I was in. I'd come to the front, and now that I could see Miss Jennings up close I thought she looked even scarier, her face was set in such a stern expression.

"Katy Parsons," I said quietly.

She smiled and nodded. "Yes, Katy, you're in Amethyst dorm." Then she looked over her glasses at Mia. "Good. You can look after Katy. Two of the others are already here." She ran her finger down the list. "So...just Georgie Henderson and Naomi Okanta still to come. Remember the code?" Miss Jennings suddenly whipped her glasses off and opened her eyes wide as if Mia was a spy who'd been captured and was getting a grilling.

"Two one two seven."

Miss Jennings nodded and said, "You'll need to remember that too, Katy. It opens Hazeldean's front door. Now, off you go."

Mia and I went across the hall toward the staircase.

"Amethyst is a jewel, isn't it?" I said.

"Yes, the sixth grade dorms in all the boarding houses are named after jewels, like Ruby and Topaz and Emerald…"

Before we reached the stairs, Dad suddenly appeared. He smiled at Mia then turned to me. I know my dad and I knew he was trying not to show he was sad. "I'll say bye then, Katy."

My throat hurt and I had to blink a lot to stop the tears from gathering.

"Here's young Buddy." Dad put down the basket and gave me a tight hug. I hugged him back and everything swam around inside my brain for a few seconds because I was suddenly confused by a vivid memory of Mom dropping me at playgroup for the very first time, and I felt like I was three years old again, crying and crying and refusing to let go of her jacket. Only now I was eleven and I mustn't cry. Not in front of Mia and the rest of the girls in this hall. But the tears were almost there and I wasn't sure that I could stop them.

Dad broke away from the hug first and pointed down at Buddy, who was wiggling around in his basket. "Think it's time he got out of there, Kates! I would get him settled in if I were you." He winked at me and squeezed my shoulder, then turned to go, and I swallowed and swallowed with all my might and clenched my teeth.

As I watched Dad go to the door, the words that Mom had said just two days ago flooded into my mind. *"If you ever feel lonely or worried about anything, you can tell Buddy all about it. He'll help you sort it out."* When she'd said that, it had made sense, but I wasn't so sure now. It didn't seem possible that one little rabbit would be able to take away this awful feeling I had. I didn't want Dad to drive home with the memory of my sad face, though, so I made a massive effort and called out, "Bye, Dad," then gave him a big smile when he turned around.

He grinned. "Talk soon, Kates."

And a second later he was out of sight. But only just, because he'd almost collided with a girl who was crashing through the doorway. She was carrying three shoulder bags and one of them was pulling her sweatshirt off her shoulder. Her face was pink from rushing, her head was bobbing around, and her eyes darted everywhere, before they suddenly settled on Mia and sparkled like crazy. Then she dropped all her bags and shrieked out, "Look! It's almost as long as yours!" And she swung her head from side to side, clouting herself in the eyes with the end of her short ponytail. Finally she rushed at Mia. "Hi! Remember me?"

Mia's eyes shone with happiness as she nodded, and introduced me. "This is Katy, Georgie."

Georgie flashed me a quick grin then bent down and started squinting at Buddy through the hole in the basket. It seemed like she was talking to him but she wasn't. "We'd better be in the same dorm, Mia, otherwise I'm going straight to Miss Carol and demanding a transfer!"

"It's okay, we're both in Amethyst, and so is Katy," said Mia.

"Good!" said Georgie to Buddy, patting his basket before jumping to her feet and eyeing me carefully. "I wish I had hair like yours," she sighed. "You look like you ought to be modeling in a hair ad. How much did you have to pay it to lie flat?"

I couldn't help laughing but Georgie wasn't expecting an answer because she was flicking her ponytail from side to side again. "See, Mia? Impressed at how fast it's grown? I've been eating buckets of yogurt for the calcium. That's why."

Mia opened her mouth to say something but Georgie was marching over to the dorm supervisor's desk, grinning all over her face. "Hello, Miss Jennings," she said in a bright voice. "Remember me?"

"How could I forget?" she said, running her finger down the list looking for Georgie's name, but I noticed she was smiling a little. "Amethyst dorm, and the Hazeldean code is two one two seven. Got that?"

"Twenty-one twenty-seven," said Georgie. "Easy! I'll be thirty in that year."

"Don't you mean a *hundred* and thirty?" asked Mia.

"Who cares? I'll be ancient anyway, so that's how I'll remember the code."

Miss Jennings raised her eyebrows and said, "Hmm," then went back to writing whatever she'd been writing before. But I was giggling like crazy because Georgie was so funny. And a moment later she was grinning and waving energetically at Miss Fosbrook, who was talking to some girls just inside the door.

"I'll be up to see how you're all getting along with

your unpacking in just a few minutes," said Miss Fosbrook, smiling cheerfully.

"We'd better take Buddy to Pets' Place first," said Mia.

Georgie rolled her eyes. "Excuse me if I don't join you," she said, wrinkling her nose. "Can't bear the smell of all those animals, you see."

Mia gave her a slightly disapproving look and Georgie immediately said, "Oops, I mean *pets*. Sorry, Mamma Mia. Anyway, my parents are coming up to the dorm with me once they've finally finished yakking away with Miss Carol."

So for the second time in under thirty seconds Georgie had made me laugh, and as I followed Mia out of Hazeldean and we walked around the back of the building toward Pets' Place, I had the feeling that maybe it was going to be all right at Silver Spires.

Chapter Two

Pets' Place is a huge shed with a yard around the back of it. There are runs in the yard for rabbits and guinea pigs, and snug little hutches with bags of hay and straw and food in the shed. I was glad that Buddy was going to be living in such a nice place, all safe and warm and smelly. Mia and I agreed that we'd come down here together to feed our pets every day.

"The caretaker told me he locks the shed when it gets dark," Mia explained, "but there's a spare key under that window."

So we introduced Buddy to Porgy and Bess, and

then put him in a hutch. I made sure he had enough hay, and kissed his head, then we went back to Hazeldean.

"I think I like Hazeldean best out of all the dorms I've seen," I told Mia. "The others don't look so warm and inviting, do they?"

Mia agreed. "I love all the vines growing up the walls."

"And the hazelnut tree at the back," I added.

We went inside and got a surprise because the hall was almost empty. Apart from Miss Carol and Miss Jennings, who were talking in low voices at the far end, there was just one girl with straight, dark brown, shoulder length hair and a golden tan, standing by the window. I guessed she was in seventh or eighth grade.

We were just about to make our way up to the dorm when I heard Miss Carol whisper the name "Naomi Okanta" to Miss Jennings. Mia must have heard too because she raised her eyebrows at me, and mouthed, "That's the other girl in our dorm. What did she say about her?"

I shrugged a *don't know* and realized at the same time that the girl by the window was sighing rather noisily. I looked at her more carefully. On her head was perched a pair of sunglasses, and around her waist was a wide studded purple belt. She had a very expensive-looking multicolored bag made of all different materials slung over her shoulder. In fact I guessed the whole outfit must have cost an awful lot. I couldn't help staring, but then she glanced in my direction and saw me looking, so I quickly smiled and asked her if she was okay.

"I'm just waiting for one of the guys to bring my trunk in," she said, in a really loud voice.

I looked to see if Miss Carol had heard but she'd disappeared and so had Miss Jennings.

"Oh...okay... What grade are you in?" I asked.

"Sixth," she said, as though it was a disease.

Mia bit her lip. "Do you know what dorm you're in?"

"Opal," the girl answered.

I wasn't sure what to do then because she was looking out of the window again, and obviously didn't want company. But then I suddenly wondered whether it was all a big cover-up because she was actually feeling miserable and homesick, so I made one more huge effort.

"I really love your outfit...especially that bag..."

And that's when she turned and looked me up and down very slowly. The tiniest shadow of a frown came over her face. "Thanks." And I felt myself blushing because it was obvious she didn't think much of what I was wearing.

"Tony is on his way, Lydia," came Miss Fosbrook's puffed-out voice. She was hurrying downstairs. "He'll take your trunk to your room. Sorry there's been a little wait." Then she saw me and Mia. "Oh, you've met Katy and Mia. That's good. You're not in the same dorm as them, but—"

"Look!"

Miss Fosbrook never got to finish her sentence because Lydia was pointing out of the window, with an astonished look on her face. "Who's that?"

"Ah," said Miss Fosbrook, hurrying to the door, "I think... Yes, it's Naomi." She turned around and shooed us all away. "Off you go, girls." Then when we all just stood there, "Off you *go*!"

But as soon as Miss Fosbrook went outside, where Miss Carol was already waiting, Lydia tossed her head and stepped out of the door behind her.

I caught a glimpse of a big black car, the length of at least two ordinary cars, and couldn't resist sneaking a look, despite Miss Fosbrook's instructions. I stayed in the doorway though, and Mia hovered uncertainly beside me. "We'd better go, Katy..." she murmured, but her eyes were wide and it was obvious she was as curious as me. "Wow!

Imagine riding around in one of those, with blacked-out windows and everything. I wonder if Naomi is famous or something."

I kept quiet about the fact that I'd been in a limousine like this one a few times with Mom, and thought to myself, *This is where it all starts – the secrets, the hiding of the truth.*

Miss Carol was beckoning to the two men who were helping with all the suitcases and trunks, and I heard the one named Tony telling the other man in a low voice that the girl arriving was a Ghanaian princess.

Mia gasped. "Did you hear that, Katy? A princess from Ghana!" Then her voice turned to a squeak. "Look, her dad's getting out!"

Lydia turned around and spoke in a don't-you-even-know-*that* voice. "It's not her father, it's the driver. We had a driver when we lived in Kenya."

Mia didn't say anything, but I saw her eyes widen as the driver went around to open the passenger doors, and at that moment Georgie appeared.

"I've been looking *everywhere* for... Oh wow!" As she stared at the car her jaw fell open.

"Naomi's a princess, Georgie," squeaked Mia. "And we're not supposed to be here, so we'd better go inside quick, before Miss Carol and Miss Fosbrook see us." She hurried off, but I stayed glued to the action. I couldn't help it.

"Well *I'm* not going inside," said Lydia. "It's no big deal, you know, being a princess in Africa. There are loads more princesses in Africa than in Europe."

Georgie made a face, jerked her head in Lydia's direction and mouthed, "Who's that?"

"Lydia," I mouthed back. On the drive, Miss Carol and Miss Fosbrook took a couple of steps forward, and out of the back of the car stepped the most beautiful girl, with a glamorous-looking woman coming out behind her.

"Is that her mom?" I whispered to Georgie.

"Obviously," Lydia answered immediately.

Georgie grinned at me. "See that? I didn't even move my lips!"

"And that will be her father," added Lydia, ignoring Georgie.

The man and woman were dressed in swirling gold and white but Naomi wasn't wearing traditional African clothes. She just looked like any of us in her jeans and top, apart from her hair, which was perfectly braided and beaded. I was certain that at any minute Miss Carol or Miss Fosbrook would turn around and see us standing there, so I grabbed

Georgie and pulled her inside. "Come on, we can watch through the window."

Georgie walked in backward so she could keep watching. "Look, shiny white suitcases!" she squeaked, as two other servants who had appeared from the other side of the car started unloading the trunk. Tony went hurrying over to them. Then Naomi's parents each gave her a peck on the cheek and said something to Miss Carol, before getting back into their car. Both the servants and the driver did small bows to Naomi and waited until she'd turned to walk away from them before getting in the car and driving off.

"Hurry up, you two," called Mia from the top of the stairs. "Miss Fosbrook will be upset if we're still hanging around when she told us to go."

"No, she won't," announced Georgie as she skipped up to the first-floor landing to join Mia, "because Naomi is in our dorm and we're the welcome party, aren't we?"

I had to admit she had a good point, so we all peered down, and I felt exactly as I had when I'd been a little girl and should have been in bed, but I'd crept onto the landing to peek at Mom and Dad's guests arriving for dinner.

And suddenly Naomi was in the hall with Lydia

right beside her, and Miss Carol and Miss Fosbrook just behind.

Lydia looked completely different when she smiled, much prettier. "I lived in Kenya for two years so I'm used to servants and everything too. My parents aren't royal like yours but they're famous," she went on.

Naomi looked at her with big eyes in a beautiful calm face but didn't say anything.

"We're not in the same dorm at the moment, Naomi," Lydia went on, "but I'm sure we'd be allowed to switch...?" She glanced at Miss Carol with her eyebrows raised in a question.

"We stick with the same dorm mates for the first part of the year, Lydia," Miss Carol said firmly, "and then in exceptional cases changes can be made." She smiled at Tony, who was taking Naomi's luggage upstairs.

"What about *my* luggage?" Lydia called out.

"Have Lydia Palmer's suitcases been taken to Opal dorm?"

"Yep," replied Tony, puffing a little as he continued walking.

"Well I didn't see—" Lydia began.

"Opal is one of the ground-floor dorms, Lydia, and there's a side entrance, which is only used occasionally," Miss Carol explained.

Miss Fosbrook put her hand on Lydia's shoulder to guide her along the corridor. "Let's go and meet your dormies."

"I'll see you at dinner, Naomi," Lydia said. "Save me a place if you get there first, yeah?"

Naomi bit her lip and nodded. Her eyes were full of confusion and everything started to click into place in my mind. I might have been wrong but I couldn't help wondering whether the reason Naomi's parents had deliberately dropped her off a little late and left very quickly was because Naomi didn't want lots of people fussing around her. A picture of Miss Carol whispering to Miss Jennings flashed through my head. That was it! That was why Miss Fosbrook had shooed Mia and me and Lydia away. I bet we weren't supposed to know that Naomi was a princess. I bet Naomi, like me, was trying to keep a big secret. But now there were four people who knew it – Lydia, Georgie, Mia and me. Poor Naomi.

I was suddenly desperate to help her guard her secret. But I could have been wrong. She might have only been looking confused because she was new and it was all a little strange. I'd better keep quiet until I found out the truth. An enormous wave of relief swept over me that I'd made the decision not to tell anyone about Mom. I had the feeling that Lydia was only acting all friendly toward Naomi, wanting to be in her dorm and everything, because she liked the idea of being friends with a princess. If she knew who *my* mom was I wonder if she'd be all over me like a rash.

Georgie went skipping down to the hall, grinning all over her face, while Mia and I followed. "Hi, Naomi, I'm Georgie. You're in Amethyst dorm with me and Mia and Katy."

Miss Carol ran a finger down one of the lists on the noticeboard. "And as well as you four, there's Grace and Jessica. They're up in the dorm, I think."

"Hi," said Naomi, smiling at all of us. She didn't look so anxious now.

"Yes," said Miss Carol, "can you three take Naomi up to Amethyst? Miss Fosbrook, Miss Jennings and I are about to do a round of all the dorms to see how the unpacking is going, then it's dinner in twenty minutes."

So up we went, Georgie in the lead. "All these steps every day are going to kill me," she said as we rounded the corner on the second landing. "If Lydia wants to switch dorms she can trade with me, any day!"

"Is this your first boarding school?" Naomi suddenly asked, sounding a little hesitant. She wasn't looking at any one of us in particular and I was the one who answered.

"Yes. It feels kind of weird at the moment."

"I'm going to have a ball!" Georgie's voice rang out loudest and made us all laugh. She went on as though she hadn't noticed. "What about you, Naomi? Is this *your* first boarding school? Do princesses go to boarding school in Africa?"

I nearly gasped. The look of shock on Naomi's face made me certain I'd guessed right about it being a secret that she was a princess, and my mind went into overdrive trying to think of a way to help her out.

"Um...I've never boarded before," she said hesitantly.

"Is it true that you're a Ugandan princess, though?" Georgie went on. I knew she was only being her usual bubbly self but I wished that she'd be quiet.

Naomi bit her lip. "Ghanaian. Only—"

"I'm going to be sleeping in the same room as a princess!" interrupted Georgie. "I can't wait to tell my friends back home."

"Georgie," I started to say, "maybe Naomi doesn't want people going on about..."

But I don't think Georgie even heard me. She was in full flow and there was no stopping her. Poor Naomi was totally embarrassed and this time I was determined to make sure I got Georgie off the subject of princesses.

"Stop talking and show us the dorm, Georgie! We must be almost there."

Georgie chuckled. "Any second now!"

I quickly turned to Naomi. "I haven't been in the dorm yet either because I was putting my rabbit in Pets' Place."

Naomi shot me a grateful smile.

"It's the next one on the right," Mia said. "We've got our own little hallway-type thing. Look!" And for a moment I forgot about Naomi and secrets as a big wave of excitement came over me. We'd rounded a corner and there was a little alcove with beams set in the walls on either side of us, and ahead of us the heavy door said *AMETHYST* at the top. Below was a list of our names. Seeing my name on the door like that made everything seem suddenly very real. My new life was starting. Right here and now. Mia turned the handle and opened the door, then the four of us piled in.

A girl with copper-colored curly hair was sitting on one of the beds cutting out pieces of newspaper with her manicure scissors. She looked up and smiled at me and Naomi. "I'm Jess and this is Grace." Grace was sitting next to Jess. She looked very slim in her jogging bottoms and a plain white top.

Georgie finished off the introductions. "This is Katy, and this is Naomi!" She tapped us both on the head. "And you've met Mia, haven't you?" Then she shot over to a cabin bed with a bright yellow comforter, and climbed the ladder. "I've got this one."

There were six beds, each one part of a unit with a desk area and drawers below, and a narrow closet at the side. Already the dorm looked like home, with all its colors and clutter. Tucked under the roof, it had a sloping ceiling on one side, and a shiny, uneven, wooden floor with rugs on it, and instead of being a plain rectangle, it had recesses which gave it a cozy feel. Naomi's and my suitcases were right in the middle of the floor.

The others had all unpacked their stuff and Grace was watching Jess sticking the pieces of newspaper onto her bulletin board to make a frame.

"You're so artistic, Jess!" she said. And I agreed.

There was a bulletin board above each of the beds and I noticed that Mia had already covered hers with photos of her family and her guinea pigs.

Georgie's stomach suddenly gave an enormous rumble, which made everyone laugh. "Quick, get unpacked you two," she said urgently. "It's got to be time for dinner soon. I'm starving."

"Um...which bed do you want?" I asked Naomi.

"You choose. You got here before me," she replied, and when I hesitated she added, "I don't mind, honestly."

My eyes couldn't help straying over to the bed tucked in a snug little alcove. "I'd love this one...as long as..."

"That's fine," said Naomi with a smile, "because I secretly preferred this one!"

I wondered whether she really did prefer it or if she was just a really kind girl.

For the next ten minutes we both worked hard. Georgie went from Naomi to me, looking at all our things as we unpacked and giving a running commentary. "Nice skirt, Katy. If my legs looked like yours I'd have to steal it from you, I'm afraid!"

When Miss Fosbrook came in we were all laughing like crazy.

"Well, this dorm gets first prize for being the merriest one!" she said. "Don't worry about sorting everything out before dinner but make sure you at least unpack everything so Tony can take your luggage down to the storage room. See you in the cafeteria in a few minutes. It's in the main building and there'll be plenty of older girls to tell you where to go if you get lost, all right?"

We all nodded and Naomi and I got straight back to work as soon as she'd gone, while Georgie peered into Naomi's jewelry case. "Wow, look at all this silver and gold! Do you have a tiara as well?"

Naomi looked embarrassed again, and my heart raced a little because I'd decided the time had come to have a word with Georgie. But as it happened Naomi got there first. She suddenly stood up straight and spoke in a firm voice, looking Georgie right in the eyes. "No, I don't have a tiara and I don't have a throne to sit on either, okay?"

Georgie swallowed and turned pink and I found myself feeling sorry for her because I knew she couldn't help being bubbly and curious. It's just her character. There was another awkward silence then Naomi sighed a big sigh. "Sorry, that came out all wrong. I didn't mean to sound horrible. It's just that I don't want anyone to think I'm different at all." She looked down and sighed again. "Because… I'm not."

"Oh come on, Naomi, you *are* different!" said Georgie, sticking her chin up. "You've got a limousine and servants and a driver. You're a princess!"

I heard Grace and Jess gasp and I tried to swallow but my mouth felt all dry.

Naomi was still looking down. "I know..." she said in a small voice. Then finally she looked up and the truth came out rather shakily. "I didn't really want anyone to know, you see..." Her eyes filled with confusion again as she turned to me. "How did you find out?"

I felt guilty and sorry at the same time. "We heard one of the men say it. We didn't know...it was a secret..."

Mia's face looked very pale. "We won't tell anyone, Naomi. We'll keep it to ourselves, won't we?" She looked around at the rest of us and we all nodded.

"Sorry, Naomi," Georgie said, looking a little sheepish. "You should have shut me up ages ago. I know I've got a big mouth."

Naomi suddenly looked relieved. "It's okay."

"But I don't get why you want to keep it a secret," went on Georgie. "If I was a princess I'd be shouting it from the rooftops. I'd love having people swarming around me, and servants bowing and everything. It'd be the coolest thing ever."

"It might be cool at first," I blurted out, "but after a while you'd wonder if people were friends with you for yourself or just because of your family."

Then I suddenly realized what I'd said and tried desperately not to blush. "I mean...I guess that's what would happen...isn't it?"

Naomi nodded hard. "Yes, that's it. And people think you're stuck-up too. That's what I had at my old school, and now I want to make a new start."

I knew exactly how she felt. It might have been *me* talking. I stood up straight to make myself feel strong. I was more determined than ever, now, to keep my own secret safe.

Chapter Three

Georgie pretended to wave a wand over Naomi. "You *shall* have a new start, Cinderella!" she declared in a warbly voice, as we all laughed. "I wish I could be as wise as you," she added. Then she must have caught sight of Grace's Olympic Games poster. "That's cool," she said, pointing.

Grace broke into a big beam and I thought how pretty she was, with her dark olive skin and shiny black hair. "I love everything to do with sports," she said shyly.

"The opposite of me then," Georgie replied, wandering over to my desk and picking up my photo of Mom and Dad. I couldn't help tensing up even though I didn't think she could possibly recognize Mom. I'd deliberately chosen a photo that had been taken on our vacation in the Alps last year, with Mom dressed from head to toe in her ski suit and wearing an enormous pair of dark glasses and a furry hood. Even though you can hardly see her face at all, the photo still reminds me of her, and that's all that matters.

"Is that your parents?" Georgie asked, looking closely and frowning hard.

But I didn't have to answer because she'd put the photo down and was looking at Mia's board.

Mia sighed. "It reminds me of home," she said quietly.

Then Georgie surprised us all by rushing over, grabbing Mia's shoulders dramatically and looking right into her eyes. "Getting homesick is strictly not allowed!" she said, imitating Miss Jennings's deep voice absolutely perfectly. Mia broke into a giggle as Georgie kicked over a blue bag by mistake. She bent down and propped it back up again. "Is this a music case?"

"Yes, I play piano," said Mia.

Georgie put her hands on her hips, pretending to be upset. "You never told me that!" Then a moment later she was back at my desk, this time with my sketchbook in her hands. "And what's this, Katy? You're not another artist, are you? How is a poor girl who's only interested in acting going to survive in a dorm with two artists, a musician, a sports maniac and a princess?" She glanced at Naomi. "Whoops! Sorry."

Everyone laughed and I tried to get my sketchbook back. "It's nothing much, really…"

But Georgie had already started flipping the pages and the others had gathered around to look.

"Fashion designs!" said Jess. "They're fantastic! I could never do anything like this."

"Me neither," said Grace. "For a start, I'm not interested in clothes."

"Not interested in clothes!" said Georgie, in high-pitched surprise. "How can you not be interested in clothes?"

"Easy," said Grace. "I spend all my time in tracksuits."

"I wish *I* looked more fashionable," said Mia, "but I'm too small!"

"No, you're not," I quickly reassured her. "I could design something that you'd look great in."

Her eyes shone. "Could you?"

"What about me?" Georgie asked. "Do you design theatrical costumes?"

I couldn't answer though because there was a loud knock on the door and as I was closest I answered it. Lydia was standing there in a completely different outfit from the one she'd been wearing earlier. She looked really glamorous in black shiny pants, suede boots with little stiletto heels and a gray and blue top. Her hair was tied back in a thick ponytail, except for two loose ringlets, one on either side of her face, and over her shoulder was the same bag she'd had earlier, only now there was a magazine poking out and I could clearly see Mom's picture was on the front cover.

My heart felt like a yo-yo for a few seconds, but then I told myself to calm down and remember no one could read my mind. I just had to act normally and make sure I didn't turn red. But even if I *did* turn red, no one would know why, as I don't particularly look like Mom. So actually I didn't have anything to worry about.

"Hi, are you coming for dinner? Everyone's on their way over to the cafeteria."

Lydia's eyes were on Naomi but it was Georgie who answered for all of us. "We'll be down in a minute."

A look of irritation flicked across Lydia's face, then she glanced around our dorm. "I think this is a little bigger than Opal." She wrinkled her nose. "But there's still not much room for all your stuff, is there?" Again she seemed to be addressing her words to Naomi only, but this time it was Jess who answered, and I could tell by the look on her face that she didn't like Lydia.

"Depends how much stuff you've got."

Lydia ignored Jess. "I'll save you a place, Naomi." Then off she went, clicking down the corridor.

"I'm starving," said Grace, making for the door. The rest of us were all following when Georgie put her hands up like a traffic cop and said, "Hold on! There's something I have to do first." She clicked her fingers at me. "Pencil, Katy!" So I went diving back to my desk to get her one, and then we all watched as she crossed out our last names from the list on the door and added some words of her own. A moment later we were grinning at her handiwork, and I was smiling inside too because it gave me that nice warm feeling that we were already becoming a kind of team – the Amethyst team.

Katy the Queen of Style
Grace the Sportswoman

45

Jess the Artist
Mia the Musician
Naomi the Princess
Georgie the Actress

Immediately we were all racing for our erasers. "Why don't you just advertise to the whole world that Naomi's a princess, Georgie!" said Jess sarcastically.

Georgie erased the word "Princess" and changed it to "Wise One," which made Naomi look a little embarrassed.

"You really are going to have to concentrate on keeping your mouth shut, Georgie!" I told her.

"Yes, and speaking of keeping your mouth shut, someone needs to tell Lydia that Naomi wants it kept secret that she's a princess," Mia pointed out.

"So she definitely knows?" asked Naomi.

I nodded.

Naomi looked thoughtful and I wondered if she was remembering how Lydia wanted to be in the same dorm as her when she'd only just met her. "I'll tell her at dinner," she said firmly.

Dinner was absolutely delicious – lamb balti followed by apple flan. All the Amethyst girls sat together and Lydia sat at the end of the table, next to Naomi. She spent the whole time telling Naomi how boring her dormies were and how much nicer she thought Amethyst dorm was.

"Um...don't forget to tell Lydia about your secret," I reminded Naomi hesitantly when she was about to go for her dessert.

"Oh yes." She gave me a grateful smile and dropped her voice. "I don't really want anyone to know I'm a princess, Lydia. It might make people act differently around me..."

Lydia's eyes shot open. "I know what you mean! It's awful when people won't leave you alone because they think you're someone important." She looked around at all of us and I could tell she was dying for someone to ask who her parents were, but the others were deep in their own conversations and Naomi was looking to see where the desserts were. The moment she'd left the table Lydia turned to me with an angry look on her face and spoke in a low, cold voice. "You didn't have to get Naomi to tell me to keep quiet about her, you know. I'm not about to spill her secret. Obviously!"

I was too shocked to reply because I hadn't meant to be bossy or anything so I mumbled something about dessert and went after Naomi.

When we'd all finished eating, the Vice Principal

of Silver Spires, Mrs. Andrews, announced that girls in sixth grade should go back to their dorms for a guided tour, followed by a meeting in the common room with the dorm parents. Mrs. Andrews also explained that Ms. Carmichael, the Head of the whole school, would be welcoming us officially to Silver Spires in assembly the next day, but right now she was over in the Senior block.

There were two guided tours of Hazeldean. I was in Miss Jennings's group with the rest of Amethyst, and Lydia, who insisted on coming with us instead of joining her own dorm. Miss Jennings told us rule after rule on the way. "Two people will be in charge of keeping the kitchen neat and if it's not neat it will be locked so you won't be able to make hot drinks for yourselves... This is the coat room for all your rain gear. Again, two people responsible for cleaning it up... You'll find the schedules on the noticeboard..." There was so much to take in. I didn't know how I'd ever remember everything. "This is the laundry room for dirty clothes. Make sure you put dark colors in here and light colors in here. See how it's all clearly labeled..." The tour seemed like a whirlwind and we were easily the first group to arrive at the big common room. Then the older girls started coming in too, for the dorm moms's talk.

Lydia dropped into the comfiest-looking chair in the room, crossed her legs and started flipping over the pages of her magazine, commenting on funky tops and glam bags, but no one was really listening to her.

"Do you feel homesick, Katy?" Naomi asked me quietly as we sat down on a sofa.

"A little," I said. "But I'm trying not to think about it too much. What about you?"

"I think I'll miss having time to myself." Her voice was soft and I felt flattered to be the one she'd chosen to confide in. "But I'll also miss my family."

"Do you have brothers and sisters?"

"Two older sisters who've gone back to Ghana, and a little brother with my parents in New York. Do you?"

"No, there's just me."

"You poor thing," said Lydia. "I've got a big family too, Naomi."

Naomi continued talking to me. "Are your parents overseas?"

I told myself to keep calm. It was only natural that everyone wanted to find out about everyone else in the first few days. It would soon be forgotten.

"My mom works in Los Angeles at the moment,

and my dad has to travel quite a lot too. But we don't live overseas."

Lydia shut her magazine and leaned forward when she heard me say that. "My mom and dad work in London. They're company directors."

My heart started beating faster now we were discussing actual jobs, but luckily I didn't have to say anything because everyone started chiming in with what their parents' jobs were. I was just feeling nice and calm when I practically had a heart attack because Georgie suddenly stabbed Lydia's magazine. "That's Cally Jamieson who plays Lee Brook! She's soooooo cool! I can't wait for *The Fast Lane*. Only five days! It's the best thing ever."

I quickly bent down and took my shoe off, then spent ages pretending my sock was stuck under my heel, pulling it up and straightening it out, while the conversation about *The Fast Lane* sizzled and sparkled around me. I had to sit back up again eventually and then I realized that the other two groups had arrived and the whole common room seemed to be buzzing with talk about the time when Lee's dog got stolen, and the look on Benny's face when he realized that Esther was wearing a wig. In no time at all every single character had been discussed, as well as half the storylines.

"I'm so glad Lee's in it more now," one girl said, and everyone agreed.

Georgie wagged a finger in the air. "Funniest person on the show," she declared firmly. "My ambition is to be as good at acting as she is."

It was so weird hearing all this talk about Mom and the other actors, who I'd met loads of times when I'd been on the set during the summer break. To everyone here they were just characters from a distant TV world, but to me they were real people. But still, I knew it would be impossible to connect me with Mom because of our different last names. Mom uses Jamieson as her professional name. My mouth felt dry and my head spun as the conversation went on.

"Are you all right, Katy? You're very quiet," Naomi whispered.

I shook my head as though bringing myself back to earth. "Sorry. I was just thinking."

Naomi must have thought I was feeling homesick because she suddenly mentioned the computer room. "It's great that we can e-mail our families any time, isn't it?"

"Here we go," muttered Georgie, seeing Miss Carol going over to stand by the TV. "Let's hope it's not too much of a lecture."

As it turned out Miss Carol just welcomed us all and went over the daily schedule. The only facts I really took in were dinner at six thirty and study hour from seven thirty until eight thirty, then free time until bed at nine. Georgie raised her hand to ask about the weekends and Miss Carol said that after Saturday morning school finished we were free for the rest of the weekend, though there were often outings and things organized for the different grades.

"I know it all seems strange and new at the moment," smiled Miss Carol, "but it'll only take a few days for you to feel as though you've been here forever!" She finished up by saying, "And girls, you all know where my apartment is from the tour. Now remember, if ever anything is worrying you, or if you simply feel like talking to someone, you mustn't hesitate to come and see me. Miss Jennings will always be in her room on the third floor, and Miss Fosbrook's room is on the first floor, so you can talk to them too if you want."

"Miss Jennings!" Georgie said under her breath. "You're joking."

Fortunately Miss Carol couldn't have heard. "Any questions?" she asked, smiling around. Then, when no one spoke, she glanced at her watch and said we had forty-five minutes until bedtime.

"Let's watch TV," said Georgie.

But pictures of Buddy kept flashing through my mind. "I think I might go and see my rabbit actually."

"I'll come too," Mia immediately said.

The sun was very low in a beautiful pink sky and everything felt so still and quiet outside after the bustle and noise of Hazeldean. Porgy and Bess whistled and wiggled as Mia cuddled them, while Buddy sat like a warm heavy cushion in my arms. As we put them back in their hutches Mia asked me if I thought I was going to like it at Silver Spires.

I was just going to say "I think so," when my head was flooded with snippets of what people had said earlier on about Mom and *The Fast Lane*. I'd thought I'd be able to simply tell a lie about Mom's job and then get on with my life without any trouble, but now I was realizing that it wasn't quite as easy as that. *The Fast Lane* was on every Friday night, and people would talk about it during the rest of the week too. I'd have to be on my guard the whole time to make sure nothing slipped out that gave my secret away. *Was* I going to like it at Silver Spires?

"I hope so," I said in a small voice.

Chapter Four

On Monday evening Naomi and I were sitting at the table in the upstairs common room with Jess, talking about all that had happened during our first school day at Silver Spires. Anyone from sixth grade through Seniors can use either of the common rooms, but most people prefer the main common room on the ground floor. The upstairs one's an L-shaped room and from the other part of the L we could hear the DVD that some older girls were watching as they drank hot chocolate and talked. Jess was busy drawing a picture of Naomi, while I was leafing through old magazines, studying the fashions.

"Is it almost done, Jess?" asked Naomi, fidgeting a little.

Jess frowned and chewed at her thumbnail. "I can't get your eyes right."

Naomi tried to hide a sigh and went back to our conversation. "What was your best part of the day, Katy?"

"Not sure. Probably...art."

"Art was totally cool!" said Jess. "I can't wait until after-school clubs start. I hope there are loads of arty ones."

"The history teacher's nice, isn't she?" said Naomi, thoughtfully.

I nodded. "I don't think I've done the homework very well, though. It's so weird having a schedule for homework and dinner and everything, isn't it?"

Jess must have decided to give up on her drawing. She pushed it across to Naomi. "It's not much good. I'll try again tomorrow."

"Not much good? It's fantastic!" I squeaked, as Lydia came into the room.

Naomi gasped and slid the picture across the table so Lydia could see it. "Isn't Jess amazing?"

Lydia hardly glanced at it. "I'm not that interested in art." Then she reached her hand out to Naomi.

"Come and see the e-mail my sister's sent me. It's so funny."

I got up too because Naomi and I had already decided to e-mail our parents once Jess had finished the picture.

"All the other computers are taken, actually," Lydia said to me.

"I don't mind waiting," I said.

When we got to the computer room, though, there wasn't a soul in sight, which made me wonder whether Lydia had just made it up about the computers all being taken, to try and put me off coming along. It was obvious from the way she always talked directly to Naomi that she wasn't interested in being friends with the rest of us. I told myself that I didn't care, but if I was honest I couldn't help feeling anxious that she might be trying to take Naomi away from our wonderful Amethyst team.

I spent the next fifteen minutes typing away as fast as I could, telling Mom and Dad my news... all about my dorm and the names of my dormies, about how nervous I'd felt at the start of every class and how anxious I'd felt when I'd gone to the bathroom between classes and then gotten lost in the main building and had to walk into French late. Mam'zelle Clemence hadn't minded at all though.

She was just worried about *me* being worried. *We have to call her Mam'zelle, instead of Miss,* I wrote, *as it's the correct French pronunciation of Mademoiselle. She's my favorite teacher, so far, partly because of her trendy clothes and her cool jewelry. In fact, she's made me feel inspired to design my own jewelry now, and there's a girl in my dorm named Jess who's going to see if she can actually make a brooch I'm designing, out of shiny paper and stuff from the art room.* I went on to tell Mom and Dad how we're allowed to use the kitchen in Hazeldean for drinks and how cozy the dorm is, how Buddy seems to have settled in, and how odd it felt waking up in a strange room with five girls I was only just getting to know.

Then I really wanted to tell them all about Naomi being a princess and all of us keeping it a secret and how I was still managing to keep my own secret. And I wanted to ask Mom how the filming was going, but Lydia was hovering just behind me and I had the feeling she might be reading over my shoulder, so I decided to save all that for a phone call, and just put, *I hope that everything is going really well, Mom, and I can't wait to hear from you soon. Lots of love, Katy.*

"Can we see what your dorm looks like, Lydia?" Naomi asked.

"It's nothing special, but I can show you my stuff," Lydia replied.

While I was sending the e-mail, my phone bleeped with a message and I saw it said *Mom* on the screen.

Thinkin bout u on day1! Bet its gr8. Luvu loads. Mom X

I tapped in my reply as we walked downstairs on our way to see Lydia's dorm. *Just emailed u. Gd so far. Nice dorm n friends. Keepin secret still! LUL. K X*

There were six beds in Opal but the room looked somehow neater than ours, partly because there weren't any recesses or sloping ceilings so it was a plain rectangle, and partly because everyone's desks were neater and no one had left any clothes spilling out of half-open drawers, or on the floor. Two girls were on their laptops and another was reading on her bed. They all said hi to us and then continued with what they were doing. Lydia jerked her head at one of the girls at her desk and mouthed the word "Boring" to Naomi, then pointed to a bed with a bright purple comforter covered in silver roses and pink hearts.

"This is my bed. And look..." She opened a drawer and pulled out a little cellophane bag with a ribbon around the top and flowers all over it. "Six Belgian chocolates!"

"You're not allowed food in the dorms," said the girl who was reading, staring at Lydia with wide, accusing eyes.

"Well the *food* won't be here much longer!" replied Lydia. She rolled her eyes at Naomi as though it was pathetic to take any notice of rules like that. "Come on, let's go, you two." And as we walked along the corridor toward the big common room she divided the chocolates out between the three of us.

"The girls in my dorm get on my nerves," said Lydia. She turned to Naomi and her eyes gleamed. "I can't wait until I get to move in with you."

I didn't like this kind of talk. I wanted to keep the Amethyst team together. "All our dormies are really nice," I quickly said.

Then Naomi looked at her watch. "It's ten to nine, you guys. We'd better go and get ready for bed."

Lydia sighed noisily as she stomped off. "It's stupidly early. I never go to bed before eleven at home."

The following afternoon it was athletics. Grace had been counting the minutes since breakfast that morning so it was no surprise that she was changed and ready before anyone else. "I don't want to waste a single second," she said, jogging in place and grinning around.

"Someone looks very fit!" said Mrs. Mellor, the PE teacher. "Do you do lots of running, Grace?"

Grace nodded. "I love it. Can I show you something?" We all stopped getting ready to see what she was pulling out of her pocket. "It's a stopwatch with a built-in speedometer and pedometer *and* milometer so you can check your speed at any time, and also tell how many steps you've taken and what distance you've run."

"What a fabulous little gadget!" said Mrs. Mellor. "My stopwatch seems very ordinary compared to that!"

Georgie groaned. "How can you be so eager Grace?" she said, making her shoulders go all droopy. I noticed that she and Jess had only gotten as far as taking off their shoes and socks and were sitting on the floor with their legs stretched out, comparing the lengths of their toes. I saw Naomi watching them too and when our eyes met a second later we both cracked up.

Lydia was standing in front of the mirror brushing her hair back but she swung around, holding her ponytail, at the sound of our laughter. "What's funny?"

"Nothing worth talking about," I said. "The moment's gone."

She let her hair drop and put her hands on her waist. "Tell me anyway."

I saw Naomi hiding a sigh. "Just Georgie and Jess comparing toes in a world of their own," she explained.

"*Thank* you," said Lydia, sounding very prim and proper. She reminded me of a teacher, the way she gave Naomi a nice smile for being the good girl who'd answered her question and flashed me an evil look in the mirror for being the naughty one. I tried not to care, but it was becoming more and more obvious that Lydia didn't like me, and I suppose that's because of Naomi and me getting along so well together.

Down on the athletics field the first thing we had to do was run around the track twice while Mrs. Mellor timed us. In no time at all Grace had gone ahead of everyone, running like a gazelle. Naomi and Lydia and a few others weren't far behind, while the rest of us followed in a bunch.

"Wait for me, you guys," moaned Georgie, from the back.

Mom and I had been jogging together quite a bit over the summer vacation and I was trying to remember what she'd told me about breathing. Gradually my legs started to feel stronger and my stride seemed to get longer because I was settling into a rhythm. Ahead of me I could see Lydia beginning to lag behind Naomi and by the time I started the second lap I'd caught up with Lydia. I was about to overtake her when I realized she was completely puffed out and had turned rather red in the face.

"Are you okay?"

"Yeah...I'm fine." She straightened up a little but I could tell she was struggling. "I'm just...taking my time...on purpose. It's bad for you...to run too fast...when you haven't been training...you know."

It sounded like she was criticizing me but I couldn't be bothered to tell her I'd been running with Mom. I just kept my eye on Grace, who'd almost finished the two laps, and on Naomi, who wasn't that far behind her.

"Come on, Katy!" yelled Naomi from the finish line a moment later. "You're doing really well!"

Grace was doing leg stretches but she stopped doing them to watch me running. "Keep it up!" she called, jumping up and down. And that made me put on a spurt.

Then Naomi held her arms out wide and stood

there grinning her head off. "Go Katy!"

I went flying into her and we hugged each other, then fell over and laughed our heads off. Mrs. Mellor tutted and rolled her eyes as we got up but I could tell she was pleased with the way we'd both run. After that she was busy marking off everyone's names on her chart and writing their timings in for them because there were a few girls all finishing at once, including Lydia, who was throwing a disapproving look in my direction.

"I hope you get that grass stain off your shirt okay, Naomi," she said.

I just ignored her. Nothing was going to spoil my enjoyment of the afternoon.

That evening we talked about how much fun PE class had been. We were in the LC, which is what we've started to call the L-shaped common room, and I was trying to design a new PE outfit, because Georgie insisted that the tracksuit we have to wear makes her feel fat, and feeling fat slows her down.

"I'd probably run faster than any of you if I was wearing the right thing," she said, nearly going cross-eyed as she tried to examine her hair for split ends.

We all laughed except Lydia, whose eyes were on the door. "Where's Naomi anyway?" she asked no one in particular.

"She'll be here in a few minutes," I told her.

Lydia's eyes flashed at me. "Yes, but where *is* she?"

"I don't know. She said she wanted to be by herself for awhile."

"Well I'm going to find her. She might be lonely."

Lydia was really annoying me. I know what it feels like to want to be alone. "I'm sure she's okay, honestly."

And at that moment Naomi walked in.

Lydia jumped up. "Are you all right?"

Naomi nodded and smiled. "I like being alone sometimes, that's all."

"I know what you mean," said Lydia. "Sometimes it's good to just get away, isn't it?"

This time Naomi gave her a really big smile as though she was pleased that Lydia understood.

Then Georgie spoke out and I couldn't help feeling pleased. "That's not what you just said, Lydia!"

"I only wanted to make sure she was okay," Lydia threw back at her. Then her arm went around

Naomi's shoulder. "Let's go and look at that website we were talking about." She guided Naomi toward the door and I got anxious again that she was just trying to take Naomi away from the rest of us. Especially me.

I was more and more convinced that Lydia was only being friendly with Naomi because she was a princess and that Naomi might get hurt if the friendship wasn't genuine, and I didn't want that to happen because Naomi's so nice. I felt as though I'd just eaten a huge meal that weighed me down so I could hardly move.

Only the weight wasn't food, it was sadness.

Chapter Five

That first week at Silver Spires went by really quickly, so there was absolutely no time to worry about my secret because of concentrating so hard on making sure I was in the right place at the right time. The teachers were mostly very kind though, and let us off if we turned up late for classes. It's so easy to get lost at Silver Spires because it's such a vast school with loads of different buildings for all the different subjects. Plus, there's the boarding houses and the sports fields and tennis courts and swimming pool complex. It's like a whole kingdom by itself.

When Friday arrived I suddenly remembered that

The Fast Lane was on in the evening and I couldn't help imagining what it would be like in the common room later with everyone talking about Lee Brook, and I broke into a sweat even though there was no way anyone could possibly guess I had any connection with Cally Jamieson. All I had to do was make sure I didn't blurt out something that would give it away, then everything would be fine.

Mom had told me in an e-mail about the filming of the new opening to the show. She said it was the very last thing to be filmed and the cast had gotten a bad case of the giggles and hadn't been able to stop laughing, so the director had made them do it again and again. Mom said it was mainly her fault because the more she tried to stop laughing, the more she couldn't. *It wasn't even funny after a while,* she'd written, *but giggles just kept sprouting out of me, and in the end the director kept filming even though I was laughing my head off and my ribs were aching, because he'd suddenly had the idea that it would work if we kept the laughter in. And it does! Wait until you see it, Kates!*

So now I was worrying that I might laugh too hard, knowing that Mom wasn't acting at all, and Lydia would turn her withering look on me and say, *You are soooo immature, Katy.* I knew that's what she thought of me because once when Georgie and I had been giggling hysterically at a joke I'd been telling, Lydia had stood there with the straightest face on earth and said it was the kind of joke that her seven-year-old brother told.

After breakfast we all went to see if the list for after-school clubs was up. They were due to start the following week, and personally I was dying to find out if there was a fashion club or anything like that.

"Gym club *and* running!" said Grace, jumping up and down. "Whoa! Cool! I'm going to go down to the field after school today and do some training."

"And music, rock climbing, cooking, chess, ballet..." Mia read out. "There are so many great clubs!"

"You can even go riding on Saturdays!" said Georgie. "Not that you'd ever catch me on a horse!"

"Art!" added Jess, stabbing the noticeboard. "Cool."

"What clubs are you doing, Naomi?" Lydia asked.

"Um...debate club, I think."

"Yes, me too," said Lydia quickly.

Unfortunately there wasn't anything like a fashion club for sixth graders, so I wasn't sure what to go for, but Mia decided on music club.

"Drama! Cool!" said Georgie. "Although really there ought to be a chill club," she went on, "where you can just sit around and chill."

And all through the day she kept on bringing it up.

"Don't you think we're overworked at this place?" she said after double math. "My idea for a chill club would definitely catch on."

"You ought to suggest it, Georgie," I told her, laughing.

Lydia rolled her eyes. "You are *sooo* immature, you two."

"What about running club?" Naomi asked me. "I'll do it if you will. We're both about the same standard, aren't we?"

"But what if all the fastest runners in the school turn up?" I said, with a shiver. "I don't want to feel totally unfit."

"Don't be silly! You're really good," said Naomi. "But seriously, we could go down after school with Grace and get some practice in."

So that's what we decided to do, and the moment the quarter to four bell went, Grace, Naomi and I raced over to the changing rooms.

"I'll time us all," said Grace, pulling out her stopwatch when we were down on the track. "If we all set off exactly together we can see how long we take."

"And see if we can beat it next time," added Naomi.

Of course Grace was the fastest, but I was pleased that Naomi and I stayed together all the way around so we made exactly the same time.

"That's because you've got the same stride and the same style of running as each other," said Grace, sounding very knowledgeable. "You're pacing each other, you see."

After that we took turns clipping the stopwatch onto our sweatpants so we could see how the pedometer worked.

"It's really great, Grace," I told her, and she looked suddenly sad.

"It's one of my most precious possessions... My great-granny bought it for my birthday before she died."

"How special that you've got this memory of her," Naomi said at once, coming out with exactly the right words to make Grace feel better. That's what I like about Naomi, she seems very wise, but it doesn't stop her from being fun.

At dinner Lydia marched up to me in the line and asked where Naomi was.

"She's just gone to the bathroom."

Lydia put her hands on her hips. "So where did you two go after school?"

"We wanted to get in training for running club."

"Well thanks for telling *me*! I was looking everywhere for Naomi." Lydia looked for a second as though she was going to explode, but then she tipped her head to the side and smiled sweetly because Naomi had appeared.

"You didn't tell me you were doing running club."

Naomi shrugged. "I like running," she said simply. "And it was fun trying out Grace's pedometer."

"It sounds really cool, Grace," said Mia. "Why don't we see how many steps we take in one day?" she went on excitedly. "I read that you're supposed to take ten thousand to stay in shape."

"That's loads!" squealed Georgie. "I'd be dead if I did that many." Then she suddenly looked excited and turned to Grace with praying hands. "All the same, dibs on wearing!"

Grace laughed and I wondered if she'd mind Georgie wearing it all day, now I knew how precious it was to her. She didn't have to make a decision then and there though, because typically Georgie had already changed the subject.

"I wish it would hurry up and be study hour!" she said.

We all stared at her. "Turning into a geek, George?" laughed Jess.

Georgie rolled her eyes at Jess. "Figure it out! The sooner we get started on homework, the sooner we finish, and the sooner we get to watch you-know-what!"

"*The Fast Lane*! Yea!" said Mia. "I'd forgotten about that."

My heart skipped a beat. *I'd* managed to forget it too, but instantly my mind filled up with emotion and little bursts of nervousness kept on hitting me all through study hour.

Afterward we gathered in the main common room and when Miss Carol came into the room and saw how many girls were wanting to watch *The Fast Lane*, she said that the Juniors and Seniors could watch it in her apartment as she was planning on watching it herself. Miss Fosbrook came and sat with us though and everyone immediately started talking to her because she's so friendly and easy to talk to. She's not really like a teacher at all.

"I didn't know you liked *The Fast Lane*, Miss Fosbrook."

"Oh yes, I'm a big fan! In fact I've got the DVD

of the first series in my room."

Georgie was sitting quietly for once, glued to the commercials, but then she flicked her eyes over to Mia. I think she was making sure Mia was okay as she'd been homesick at night quite a few times lately. Georgie's such a sweet person, even if she is a little nuts. She's always the one to give Mia hugs and brighten her up.

And that was the thought I was having when she suddenly shushed everyone in the common room very dramatically. "Silence in court! It's on! It's on! *The Fast Lane* is about to begin!"

My heart started pounding and I wished I wasn't sitting wedged in between Naomi and Georgie because surely they'd feel how tense I was. And of course that thought made me even tenser. Then the music started and the very first picture was a close-up of Mom laughing hysterically, and the whole common room burst out laughing and didn't stop all through the opening, it was so funny. I didn't have to worry about the little tears of pride that pricked the corners of my eyes, because no one was paying any attention to me at all and even if they had been, they'd just think I was crying with laughter.

Once the opening sequences stopped and the actual story began there was no sound in the common room apart from explosions of laughter erupting all over the place. But I had another shock when I suddenly recognized some of the lines that the characters were saying, and realized that I'd actually tested Mom on parts of this program during the summer vacation. That made me hot and tense, so it was a relief when it came to the commercials.

"I'd love to be like Lee," sighed Mia, which started everyone else off saying who their favorite character was.

"But Lee's definitely the best actress," said Georgie, which made me feel really proud of Mom. "She's just so totally believable. Can we borrow your DVD tomorrow afternoon, Miss Fosbrook?"

"There's a shopping trip tomorrow afternoon, remember," Lydia cut in. "Why don't you just *buy* the DVD?" she asked in her loud voice. She was looking at Georgie as if to say, *How can you not have figured that out?*

"Because we're not all made of money," Georgie answered.

"They only cost—" began Lydia, but she was interrupted by a huge "Sssshhhhh!" from just about everyone in the room as *The Fast Lane* was back on again.

The second half was even better than the first

half and I got so wrapped up with the storyline that I actually managed to relax. After it had finished, while everyone was talking excitedly, I went off to text Mom.

U were great! Big hit at SS! Miss u. Luv u K X

And the reply came back almost immediately.

Bet ure the only girl at SS who gets to see her Mom once a week! Love you. X

I was smiling to myself about that as I went back into the common room. A few girls had gone off to their dorms, but the rest were still buzzing about *The Fast Lane* and Georgie told me she was planning on saving up for the DVD.

"Well I'm going to get it tomorrow," said Lydia, "and if you're really good I'll let you watch it with me!"

"Yea!" said Georgie, waltzing Mia around the common room. "Just think, only Saturday morning school to get through, then shopping and freedom right until Monday morning. Fantastic!"

Naomi suddenly looked really fed up. She beckoned us all to come closer and spoke in a whisper. "My parents have arranged for me to do an interview for a magazine on Saturday afternoon, so I can't come on the shopping trip. I tell you, I'm furious with them."

"Oh, you're so famous, Naomi!" hissed Georgie.

"Ssh!" I quickly said.

Georgie glanced around. "No one heard."

"Is it at school?" asked Mia.

Naomi nodded. "In Miss Carol's apartment. That's the trouble. Mom and Dad just don't realize how important it is to me that no one finds out I'm a princess."

"What's the magazine?" asked Lydia.

"It's called *Family*, so it's not one that anyone here is likely to read, thank goodness."

"Will they take photos?" asked Georgie, her eyes getting bigger by the second.

"S'pose so. They usually do," said Naomi, looking more fed up than ever. "I just wish I wasn't missing the shopping trip, but the interview was arranged ages ago so I absolutely have to do it."

Lydia put her arm around Naomi. "Don't worry, I'll stay behind so you're not all by yourself. I can get the DVD next week."

"That's really nice of you, Lydia, but you don't have to, honestly. It'll be boring for you."

"It's okay, really. I'll just sit in the corner and be as quiet as a mouse..." She put on a naughty smile. "...unless they want any photos of Princess Naomi's friend!"

"Oh yes!" squeaked Georgie. "Group picture!

Group picture! We'll all be in it!"

Naomi rolled her eyes. "No way! People might start asking questions about why you're not going shopping, when you've been going on about it all week."

"One friend would be okay, though, wouldn't it?" said Lydia, looking very serious now.

I could see Naomi hesitating. "Well..."

Lydia grabbed her hand excitedly. "Let's ask!"

"No, sorry," said Naomi firmly. "I really want to keep it quiet. I'll just do it on my own."

Miss Fosbrook suddenly appeared and everyone looked over, so I think I was the only one who noticed the sour look on Lydia's face.

Later, when I was brushing my teeth with Naomi, she suddenly did a huge sigh and spoke to me in the mirror. "If I was going to have *anyone* in a magazine photo with me, I'd have chosen you, Katy..."

I felt so happy at that moment. "Thank you, Naomi! That's really cool."

"To tell you the truth," she went on thoughtfully, "I don't know what to think about Lydia. Sometimes she's really nice and friendly, like she was just then, offering to stay back from the shopping trip to keep me company, but then I wonder whether it's just so she can have her photo taken with me."

I thought about the way Lydia is only ever nice to Naomi and isn't interested in being friends with the rest of us at all, and I felt like blurting out, *I'm sure it's only because you're a princess,* but I managed to stop myself. It might have been hurtful to Naomi to hear someone actually saying what she was suspecting. So instead, I put my arm around her and told her I'd bring her a surprise back from the shopping trip.

"Hey, cool! I love surprises!"

And that's another thing I've got in common with Naomi, I thought to myself as I lay snuggled up in bed that night, planning what to get her.

Chapter Six

I was so excited about going shopping – all those fantastic new clothes shops to see. But it felt a little weird going in a minibus. There were two school buses, because so many sixth graders wanted to join the shopping trip. The older girls were allowed to catch the bus on their own and I was looking forward to when that would be me. Miss Fosbrook came in our minibus with the dorm mom from Oakley, Miss Bromley. They sat at the front near the driver and talked all the way into town, apart from turning around occasionally to tell everyone to quiet down. Georgie, Mia and Grace were all the way at the back, and Lydia was somewhere in the middle, but Jess and I were right behind the dorm moms. We were probably the only quiet ones on the bus, because I was concentrating on trying to draw a pair of shoes and Jess was watching.

"You're really good at art, Katy," she said after awhile.

"No I'm not. I can only draw clothes and shoes! And on this bumpy ride I can hardly draw anything!"

Then we both clearly heard Miss Fosbrook say to Miss Bromley, "They've been caged up all week, it's no wonder they're going berserk!"

"Caged up?" said Jess quietly to me. "Anyone'd think we were animals! Can I borrow a page of your sketchbook? I want to try something out."

"Who's that girl sitting by herself staring out of the window?" I heard Miss Bromley asking quietly. "She doesn't look very happy."

Miss Fosbrook turned around. "That's Lydia Palmer." She lowered her voice. "Miss Carol had some visitors this afternoon and I saw Lydia talking to one of them. She was all smiles at first but then she turned scowly and now she's just plain sulking. I don't know *what* that's about!"

Jess looked at me wide-eyed and whispered,

"Do you think Lydia actually went and talked to the magazine people, even after what Naomi said last night about wanting to do the interview by herself?"

I nodded, thinking that would explain why Lydia had gone rushing off after lunch.

"I knew she was lying about wanting to do her hair when she had loads of time to get ready for the shopping trip," hissed Jess. She dropped her voice. "Hey, do you think she had the nerve to ask to be in the photo with Naomi?"

I shook my head. "No. That would have made Naomi angry."

"So why was she looking scowly then?"

I shrugged. "Maybe the magazine people were too busy to talk and told Lydia to go away or something."

Jess nodded and we fell silent for the rest of the journey. When we got to the town square Miss Fosbrook shushed us all and explained the rules. "Now girls, you need to show me that you can behave responsibly and sensibly. We'll meet up here in an hour and a half by the fountain. Make sure you always stay with at least one other person, and call me if you have any problems." Then she smiled, and added, "And don't spend too much money. This is only the first weekend of school, remember!"

Two minutes later I was in a shoe store, trying on the best pair of shoes ever.

"They're totally awesome, Katy!" said Georgie. "Why don't you buy them?"

"No way. I'm not blowing my allowance on a pair of shoes!" I told her.

"You don't even know how much they cost," she said, bending down and lifting up my right foot, which made me lose my balance so I had to hop a little. "Stand still, for goodness' sake, Katy!"

"I'm trying!" I laughed.

"Stop being so immature, you two," said Lydia, picking up an identical shoe off the display. "One hundred and thirty dollars."

Georgie let my foot drop. "Ridiculous!"

"Well that settles it," I said, taking the shoe off. "It's far too much."

Lydia made a face. "Surely your parents would give you an extension to your allowance?"

"No, they'd get onto me for wasting money on something I didn't really need."

"That's exactly what *my* parents would say," said Georgie. "Come on, folks! Clothes stores next. Where shall we start? Abercrombie?"

But I'd spotted a thrift store on the other side of the street. "That's where I'm going," I said, pointing.

"Why?" asked Lydia.

"It's fun seeing if there are any bargains," I explained.

I heard Lydia say "Weird" under her breath, and when the rest of us went in, she stayed outside. I found a beautiful dark-brown scarf with sequins on it that I bought for a dollar fifty, and as soon as we were out of the store I wrapped it around my hips.

"That looks so cool!" said Jess.

Next we went to the bookstore and I spent ages finding a really good joke book for Naomi. "This'll cheer her up after missing the shopping trip," I said, giggling to myself as I read through the jokes on the first page. Georgie got a book for her little sister's birthday, then we spent ages in the candy shop where everyone except Grace bought candy.

"I'm getting this for Naomi," said Lydia, picking out an enormous box of chocolates. "This is the way to cheer her up. *You'll* see."

I couldn't help feeling annoyed because I was sure she'd only thought of buying a present for Naomi because *I* had.

After that we went to a few more stores. Georgie bought a scrunchie and two headbands, but Lydia bought three things – the DVD of *The Fast Lane,* a pair of socks with toes in them and a sparkling silver and green scarf.

"I'll wear this around my hips when I've got my shiny black pants on," she told us as we left the boutique. "It doesn't really go with jeans." She gave me a look, but I couldn't tell whether the look was saying that I had no taste, for putting my scarf with jeans, or whether it meant that her scarf was better quality than mine so it needed to go with something fancier. I sighed to myself, wishing that Naomi could have heard what Lydia just said, so she'd realize that she's not actually a very nice girl. But somehow, Lydia never makes comments like that in front of Naomi.

"Haven't you spent a lot?" Jess asked Lydia, once we'd grabbed the best table at the coffee shop and were sitting around it on the squishiest sofas ever.

"My parents said they'll send me more money whenever I need it," Lydia explained. "They just want me to be happy."

"You lucky thing," said Georgie. "Are your parents really rich then, Lydia?"

"Yes, they both earn loads."

"My dad earns quite a lot," said Georgie, "but Mom only works part-time. I think it's taken all their money to pay for me to come to Silver Spires.

They were hoping I might get a scholarship but we can't all be gifted like Mia."

"What, so you got a scholarship?" Jess asked Mia.

Mia turned pink and looked down. "Only a music scholarship, not an academic one."

Georgie put her arm around her. "You see, she's modest as well as gifted. Which is something else I'll never be, by the way."

"But you are the *wittiest* person here," I pointed out, and Georgie went all theatrical and blew me a kiss across the table as everyone laughed. "Well, thank you, Katy!"

"What about *your* parents, Grace?" asked Georgie. "I suppose they must be pretty rich sending you to a school in America when you come from Thailand."

Grace looked embarrassed. "Well...um... actually... I got a sports scholarship."

Georgie groaned. "Why is everyone so talented? It's not fair!"

"Well Naomi and I aren't particularly talented," said Lydia. "We're just lucky because we're..." She faded off and flicked her eyes around the room as though she'd suddenly let out a secret by mistake.

"Well, come on," said Jess. "We all know that

Naomi's a princess. What are you?"

I must admit I was feeling curious myself.

"It doesn't matter," said Lydia, with a kind of secretive smile.

"Let me guess," said Georgie. "A countess? A dukess?"

"Duchess!" we all corrected her.

"No, nothing like that," said Lydia. "It's just that...I've only ever talked to Naomi about this before because she understands...but my parents own a massive advertising company. Everyone's heard of it in Europe. So Mom and Dad are really well known over there. We've lived in London for years."

Georgie leaned forward, wide-eyed. "You mean they're famous? Do people, like, recognize them?"

Lydia nodded and smiled around at us. "It's no big deal, but now you see why I get along with Naomi so well. I mean, I've had to do interviews and stuff in Europe as well..."

I saw a look of irritation flash across Jess's face. "Well, I'm nothing special because I didn't get a scholarship and neither of my parents are famous. In fact they're both accountants, which everyone says is the most boring job in the whole world!"

My heart pounded because my moment had

come and I knew I had to collect my words and tuck them in quickly underneath Jess's so as not to draw attention to myself. "Well my dad produces documentaries for videos, and..." I braced myself for the lie. "...My mom's a set stylist, which is—"

"It's when you have to arrange a room in a certain way so it can be photographed for magazines and things," interrupted Lydia. "I know that because Mom often employs stylists to work for her." Her eyes suddenly lit up. "Hey, wouldn't it be funny if my mother had ever employed *yours*!"

Lydia always had to be the most important person, but it was annoying me more than ever now that she was suggesting her mom was better than mine. I couldn't reply, though, even if I'd known what to say, because Georgie was making loud noises with her straw, sucking up the very last of her mocha smoothie. We all had to tell her to be quiet because people were looking.

"Well I think it must be cool to be a set stylist," said Mia. "That's probably why you're so good at art, Katy. You get it from your mom."

It was a sweet thing to say but it wasn't true. "Jess is tons better than me." Then I remembered something. "Hey, can we look at the drawing you did on the bus, Jess?"

She wrinkled her nose. "It's not finished…"

"Doesn't matter," said Grace, leaning forward.

Jess pulled the page from my sketchbook out of her bag and laid it on the table, and the hairs on my arms stood up. She'd drawn a cage at a zoo with animals squashed up tight inside it, but you couldn't really tell what kind of animals they were because they were all standing up on their hind legs and their heads were pressed together so you couldn't see their faces.

"I don't get what it is," said Lydia.

"Is it at a zoo?" asked Georgie.

"Jess and I heard Miss Fosbrook saying to Miss Bromley that we were being loud on the bus because we'd been caged up all week," I explained. "It's really great, Jess," I added.

"Are they supposed to be animals or people?" asked Lydia.

"It doesn't matter what they are," said Grace, picking the picture up slowly and staring at it with big eyes. "It's just a feeling about being caged up."

Jess's whole face lit up at those words and she asked Georgie to trade places with her so she could sit next to Grace, so while the rest of us finished up our drinks those two were deep in conversation together.

"Let's go," said Georgie, looking at her watch. "I want to zip to that new gift shop we spotted before we have to be at the fountain. Come on, Mamma Mia!"

On the minibus on the way back I sat next to Lydia because Jess was with Grace. I was working on my shoe designs while Lydia was busy texting away.

She glanced over with a bored look on her face at one point. "You're obsessed with drawing shoes." Then her phone bleeped and she scanned the screen quickly. "Text from Naomi. She finished her interview ages ago and now she's exploring the school."

A moment later I got a text too. All it said was *Cant w8 2cu. Sthing bads happened. Nao x*

"Who's it from?" Lydia asked, trying to peer over my shoulder.

I quickly deleted it. "Same message as yours," I said, thinking fast. "Naomi must have sent it to both of us at the same time."

Then, as Lydia buried herself in yet more texts, I looked out of the window. It had started to rain and the grayness made me go into a daydream all the way back, wondering whatever could have happened to Naomi. I was expecting to see her the moment I jumped off the minibus, but there was no one in sight at Hazeldean.

"I'm going to find Naomi," Lydia said, making for the common room.

We all followed and kind of exploded through the door. There were loads of girls in there but no sign of Naomi.

"Have any of you seen Naomi?" asked Lydia.

"No, but guess *what*!" said a girl named Steph, eyes sparkling. "She's a princess! It's true, honestly! Naomi Okanta is a princess!"

"What?" I managed to squeak. But I knew I'd heard her all right. I just couldn't believe the news was out.

It came as a shock when Lydia's voice rang out. "Yeah, we know. Naomi told her close friends ages ago, but we've been keeping it a secret." She turned and looked at the rest of us. "Haven't we?"

Every one of us nodded dumbly, and I expect we were all thinking the same thing. How had the secret been leaked?

Jess was the one who broached the subject. "So how did you guys find out?" she asked, and I held my breath.

Steph frowned then turned to the girl next to her. "It was *you* who told me. How did you find out?"

The girl shrugged. "Dunno. Everyone was just saying it down at the pool."

"I'm going to find Naomi," I mumbled, making my way toward the door.

Lydia pushed past me. "Me too."

And we left the others talking loudly, trying to untangle the mystery of exactly who told who. Neither of us said a word as we raced up the three flights of stairs to Amethyst and I pushed open the door. Naomi was lying on her bed. She looked as though she'd been crying and I wanted to give her a tight hug, but somehow Lydia got there first.

"You poor thing," she said, clutching Naomi's hand. "I can't believe the secret's out." She hesitated for a moment, then asked, "Do you know how it happened?"

Naomi shook her head as she sat up. "I just don't get it."

"How long have you been up here by yourself?" I asked her quietly.

"Not long. I took a walk around first."

"Well, I'm going to dump my bag in Opal," said Lydia, brightening up all of a sudden. "But first…" She pulled out the box of chocolates with a flourish. "Da-daaaaa! These are for you, Name! I thought they'd cheer you up as you missed the shopping trip."

Naomi's face lost its anxious look for a moment as she took the chocolates and gave Lydia a hug. "Hey, thanks. That's really nice of you." Then she suddenly noticed my new scarf. "That looks nice, Katy? Where did you get it?"

"The Cancer Research shop. I like getting things from thrift stores..."

"Me too," said Naomi, "because you save money and you know the money you're spending is going to help someone too."

I nodded hard because that was exactly what *I* thought, but Lydia stared at Naomi as though she was talking double Dutch, then suddenly she tapped the chocolate box and said, "I would have made it an even bigger one if I'd known you were having such a bad time here." She practically skipped out of the door. "Back in a sec. Don't move a muscle!"

As soon as she'd gone Naomi wrinkled her nose. "I don't like the name, 'Name'!"

"Why, because it's not a real name?" I asked, which set us off giggling.

Then her face clouded over.

"What exactly happened?" I asked her quietly.

She sighed. "Well, I did the interview with a woman journalist and I had my photo taken loads of times by a photographer. Then both the magazine people went, and I talked with Miss Carol for about five minutes. She was really nice, just asking me how I was settling in and whether I felt that I'd made any good friends and I told her I'd made quite a few and everything was fine. After that, I decided to go over to the library and when I was there some eighth grade girls asked me if it was true that I was a princess, and I asked them how they knew that and they said they'd heard some other girls talking about it, but they didn't know what grade they were in. And then on my way back some seventh graders started asking me how it felt having a king for a dad and things like that. By the time I got back to the common room all of Hazeldean seemed to know, so I went to Miss Carol and it was obvious she was totally shocked."

"What did she say?" I asked.

"She said she was baffled because everyone was at lunch when the magazine people arrived with their cameras and stuff, and there was no one around at all when they were leaving because people were either out shopping or they'd gone swimming or something. So they couldn't be the reason why everyone knows."

Suddenly, I knew I had to tell Naomi what I'd heard on the minibus. "Well, on the way into town,

I heard Miss Fosbrook telling Miss Bromley that she saw Lydia talking to Miss Carol's visitors. She said Lydia was being all smiley at first but then turned sulky."

Naomi gasped. "Talking to the magazine people! But I said I wanted to do it on my own, and everyone should go on as normal." She sighed again. "She must have talked to them at the end of lunch when she said she was going to do her hair. But that still doesn't explain how everyone knows my secret, does it?"

I didn't say anything, and I was just trying to figure out why Lydia had been in a sulk, when she suddenly appeared in our dorm, looking amazing in her black shiny pants with the new scarf tied around her hips.

"Lydia, did you—?" began Naomi, but Lydia interrupted her.

"Have you started the chocolates yet?"

"No...but—"

"Good, because I was thinking we ought to have a midnight feast in your dorm. If we all sneak something out of the cafeteria for the next few meals, we'll have plenty of stuff. And I'll bring my bottle of fizzy passion-fruit juice. I've been saving it for a special occasion, but this *is* special, isn't it, because we've got to cheer you up, Name!"

After that, Naomi mustn't have felt like confronting Lydia about talking to the magazine people. It might have seemed a little mean when Lydia was being so nice. And for the rest of the day whenever people clustered around asking Naomi what it was like being a princess, Lydia was right there, practically glued to her side, shooing people away and telling them Naomi simply wanted to be left in peace. "Look, just leave her alone. It's really annoying having people going on and on about it when you're well known." And then of course everyone wanted to know how Lydia knew what it was like to be well known, so out came the story about her parents being famous in Europe. She was really showing off, but it was true that she was getting the attention away from Naomi at the same time, which Naomi seemed relieved about. She kept on flashing Lydia grateful smiles.

The rain didn't stop until dinner time, and the more the day got grayer and grayer, the more my spirits sank. Lydia was telling Naomi about the shopping trip, but they were too far away for me to join in. I sat at the end of the table poking at my food, while Grace and Jess were taking photos of each other on their cell phones on one side of me, and Georgie was comforting Mia on the other side, because Mia's piano practice hadn't gone very well.

Then an older girl passed our table and I saw her jerk her head at Lydia and Naomi and say to her friend, "Birds of a feather flock together, eh?" I'd heard that saying before. It meant it was no wonder Lydia and Naomi hung out together, because they had a lot in common.

That was when I felt a horrible anxiety creeping slowly up on me. I'd only been at Silver Spires one week but already a pattern was emerging.

Georgie and Mia.

Grace and Jess.

Naomi and Lydia.

I shivered. Where did that leave me?

Chapter Seven

Hazeldean was suddenly very popular. It didn't matter what day of the week it was, there were always sixth and seventh grade girls from other boarding houses hanging around. It was obvious they were just looking for Naomi, but they were usually disappointed because she was so rarely there. I was never sure where she'd slipped off to, and I didn't ask her. Georgie and Lydia did though, and Naomi would answer vaguely that she'd just been "around."

Lydia would stand in the hall with a crowd of people around her and act like a teacher explaining to a bunch of little kids that Naomi was perfectly normal – just like any of them – all the time she was at Silver Spires. It was only at home that she had servants bowing to her and people flocking around and taking her photo and so on. Then she'd look all coy and add that that was something you just got used to. I couldn't imagine that Lydia had servants who bowed to her, because why *would* they? But when I actually asked her that question she snapped at me that I'd never understand because it was way off anything I'd ever been used to. I'd had to bite my tongue to stop myself from coming back with a couple of facts about exactly what I *was* used to. Lydia just loved all the attention though, and now people were even more interested because they could talk about a princess with a famous best friend.

One time when Naomi had been away for over two hours, she came back to find Hazeldean nice and quiet.

"You'll be pleased to know I've gotten rid of all your fans!" said Lydia.

Naomi gave her a grateful smile. "Thanks, Lydia. It's really kind of you."

"That's okay," Lydia replied, linking her arm through Naomi's. "All this fuss'll soon die down, you'll see."

I went to bed feeling kind of miserable again that

night, worrying that I was getting pushed away from Naomi. But the next day I opened my eyes to find the dorm lit up with bright golden sunlight that slanted through the curtains and cast moving shadows on the walls and the floor. Immediately my spirits lifted, and I made a resolution to stop getting obsessed about being left out of friendships.

Naomi opened her eyes as I was having that thought and turned straight to me.

I grinned at her. "Isn't it pretty and bright?"

She nodded and stretched, then looked suddenly happy. "Debate club today! Great!"

"You must be out of your tree," said a drowsy voice.

"Go back to sleep, George!" I laughed. But I had to agree with her, it wasn't *my* first choice of clubs either. "I might go exploring," I went on, feeling excited because there were lots of parts of the school I hadn't seen yet. Then I thought of something even better. "Grace, can I borrow your stopwatch after school? I want to see what distance it is from one end of the school grounds to the other."

Naomi sat up suddenly. "I'll take you on a guided tour! I know all of the school grounds now!" Then she made a face. "Oh…but I've got debate club…"

By morning break she'd decided to skip debate club and come with me instead. "There's one place I'm dying to show you," she whispered. "My secret place."

It was French after break but I couldn't concentrate very well because I kept thinking about exploring with Naomi and seeing her secret place. Then roughly halfway through the class we were reading a passage about the Paris fashion show, and I suddenly had a massive urge to draw a jacket with lots of intricate detail. I thought I'd be able to listen to Mam'zelle Clemence at the same time if I kept the sketchbook on my lap and only added a part to the design when I was certain she wasn't looking, but I made the mistake of thinking she was tied up helping someone at the front, and didn't notice her coming over to my table until it was too late. Mam'zelle Clemence pointed to the book in my lap and went crazy.

"What is *zat*, Kateeee!" she demanded loudly.

I handed it over with a red face, feeling everyone's eyes on me. Her face was screwed up in a disapproving frown but then, miraculously, the frown began to melt and she nodded slowly. "Hmmm, nice drawing. Did you copy zees?"

I shook my head. "No...it's my own..."

"Hmm. I like eet." Then her frown came back as she dropped the book on my table. "Howeverrr, eeet is not to rrree-appear in ze French class, hmmm?"

The others thought Mam'zelle Clemence sounded so funny that they kept on imitating her all through the day, especially Georgie. "Hmmm, I like eet. Deed you copy eet?" Naomi joined in as much as the rest of us at first, but by lunchtime she seemed too fed up to bother because she was being pestered again by people wanting to talk to a princess.

It was when we'd finished our first course that she suddenly surprised me by turning to Lydia and blurting out, "Did you talk to the magazine people that day I had my interview, Lydia?"

There was an awkward silence. Georgie stopped like a statue with an open mouth and a forkful of food about to go in it. Jess and Grace broke off their conversation to listen.

Lydia tossed her head. "No, course I didn't. And even if I did, what difference would that have made?"

"Well, Miss Fosbrook said you did," I couldn't help myself saying.

A second later I felt myself shrinking under Lydia's cold gaze. "Look, all I did was answer when the photographer spoke to me. Terribly sorry, Katy, but I didn't realize that was against the law," she said sarcastically. I felt myself blushing as she shut her eyes slowly then opened them and went on in an over-the-top patient voice. "Miss Carol's door was open. The photographer saw me passing and asked me if lunch had finished and I said it was just finishing and that Naomi would be along in a moment. He also asked me if Naomi was a friend of mine and I said that she was. Anything wrong with that, Katy?"

I shook my head and felt a fool.

"I'm only trying to find out how everyone found out about me," said Naomi quietly, "and I wondered if you might have said the word 'princess' by mistake and someone might have heard."

"Well, I didn't!" snapped Lydia. Then she leaned in closer to Naomi. "I'd be the last person to give your secret away," she smiled. "Surely you know that by now."

I was probably the only one who saw the nasty look Lydia flung at me as she straightened up and calmly continued eating.

At the end of school Grace gave me and Naomi her stopwatch and we headed straight for the Senior block, which was 848 steps away. Then Naomi took me on a path that went behind some trees and we came out at the other side of the athletics track, which was where she suddenly clapped her hand to her mouth and said, "Oh no! I forgot to tell Lydia I wasn't going to debate club. She'll wonder where I am!" A shadow crossed Naomi's face, then she shrugged and mumbled, "Oh well, never mind."

There was no one at all on the athletics track and it looked so tempting that we decided to run around it.

"Hang on a sec!" I said taking my sweater off. "I've got a better idea. Let's do it three-legged!"

Naomi giggled as I tied my sweater around our ankles. "The pedometer will probably have a heart attack!"

We set off far too fast and fell in a heap laughing our heads off, and that's when I heard the dreaded voice and looked up to see Lydia standing over us, making a face as though she'd just come across a pile of dog poo. "What *are* you doing?" She was looking at me and sneering, but then she spoke to Naomi in a lighter voice. "Where did you go to? I thought we were supposed to be doing debate club."

"I know...sorry," Naomi replied, scrambling to her feet, which wasn't easy with one of her ankles tied to mine. "I forgot to tell you I...changed my mind."

Lydia turned her gaze on me and I saw real jealousy in her eyes, which made me shiver it was so strong, but she recovered quickly and smiled at Naomi. "Actually I'm fed up with debate club so I've signed us both up for rock climbing next week."

"Oh no! I'm not very good with heights!" said Naomi.

"You'll be okay. And anyway, I can help you," said Lydia, linking her arm through Naomi's as we all started walking back to Hazeldean.

I felt my spirits sinking, but I remembered my resolution not to let Lydia bother me. I just wished nothing had interrupted my fun time joking around with Naomi. Now I wouldn't even get to see her secret place.

"Too bad you can't wear Grace's pedometer when you're climbing," I laughed, trying to keep our fun alive for a minute longer. "Maybe it would tell you how high you've gone!"

Naomi grinned at me but Lydia rolled her eyes.

"That's stupid. Of course it wouldn't. You'd just end up breaking it," she said.

"Well anyway, I think it's great. I'm going to ask for one for Christmas and get in some training at home. Then, when I come back after the holidays I'll be in even better shape than Grace!"

"Like *that* would happen," said Lydia under her breath. She was looking at me as though I'd announced I was going to get a crown so I'd be just like Naomi.

"I was only joking," I told her a little snappily. "I'm not that big on running. I much prefer fashion design."

"Oh yes," said Lydia, very bright all of a sudden. "That reminds me, I came across Mam'zelle Clemence, and she wants you to go and see her about starting a fashion club."

"A fashion club! Great!"

"She lives at Oakley. She said she'd be on duty all evening."

I was surprised that Lydia was being so helpful all of a sudden, but pleased too, and I couldn't wait to talk to Mam'zelle Clemence.

Miss Fosbrook let us out of study hour really early because for once everyone had found it pretty easy, so I went straight over to Oakley. I asked someone where Mam'zelle Clemence was, but it turned out that it was her evening off, so there was nothing I could do but go back to Hazeldean, wondering irritably whether Lydia had deliberately lied to me or Mam'zelle Clemence had just forgotten she wasn't on duty that evening.

When I found my friends in the LC, they were sitting around the table playing cards.

"What did Mam'zelle Clemence say?" asked Naomi as soon as she saw me.

"She wasn't there. I guess I'll see her tomorrow."

"Oh." Naomi looked surprised. "Anyway, come and join in."

"She can't. It's for pairs," Lydia pointed out.

My thoughts were racing. Maybe I was getting paranoid, but I couldn't help wondering whether this was Lydia's latest way of making sure I was excluded from the group.

"It's okay, I'll watch," I quickly said. "What do you have to do?"

"We've all invented a secret signal with our partner," Jess explained. "You have to keep trading your cards in until you get four that are all the same and then give your partner the secret signal without anyone detecting it..."

I watched them playing for about ten minutes,

then Naomi insisted that I join in. "You can be Lydia's partner," she said. "I don't mind watching, honestly."

"But then Katy will know our signal," said Lydia.

"You could invent a new one," Jess suggested.

But Lydia seemed to have other plans. "*Or*," she said dramatically, "we could watch my DVD of *The Fast Lane*!"

"Yea!" said Georgie. "Good thinking!" And she leaped up from the table.

Some other sixth graders were in the middle of watching a program on TV. They said we'd have to wait until it was finished, but when they saw that Naomi was one of the people wanting to watch the DVD they instantly changed their minds and all patted the seats next to them, grinning at Naomi and encouraging her to sit down.

"Leave her alone," said Lydia. "She's sitting with me." Then she flopped back into the biggest beanbag and pulled Naomi down with her.

The episode we watched was the earliest one of all, so Mom wasn't in it until over halfway through because this was when she was new to the show. As soon as she came on I was filled with the memory of the first time she'd had to go to L.A. I was eight and I'd been staying with my grandparents because Dad was away too, and I could clearly remember how my granddad had been sick and I'd not been allowed to make any noise around the house. The whole place had seemed really sad and still, and I'd felt lonely because Grandma was too busy taking care of Granddad to bother with me.

After the episode finished I couldn't stop thinking about it all and I was desperate to talk to Mom. I tried and tried to get through on the phone but wasn't having any luck. I was standing at the end of the first-floor corridor because it's very private just there and the reception is good. It was dark and stormy outside and the rain was beating against the window. I could hear rumbles of thunder too, which usually makes me feel cozy when I'm safely in the warm and dry. But not today. A horrible sadness was gradually seeping its way inside me as I kept going over the show in my head and picturing Mom's face, and remembering how lonely I'd been at Grandma's.

If I pressed my nose to the windowpane I could just about see Pets' Place in the distance. The shed has a corrugated iron roof and the rain must sound like bullets hammering down, to the animals inside. Poor Buddy. I wondered if he was frightened. And as

I stood there staring out at the darkening sky an idea began to take root in my mind. What was it Mom had said? *If you ever feel lonely or worried about anything, you can tell Buddy all about it. He'll help you figure it out.* Yes. That's what I'd do. I'd go and see Buddy. But I'd have to be careful because everyone would be getting ready for bed any minute now, and Miss Jennings was on duty. I'd be in big trouble if she found me going out at this time. We're not allowed out of the boarding house after eight thirty and the door is locked at nine.

I hurried downstairs and passed Miss Carol at the bottom, so I pretended to be going toward the common room.

"Almost bedtime, Katy," she said, looking at her watch.

"I left something in the…"

"Okay, quick as you can." Then she was gone, heading toward her apartment.

No one else was in sight so I dashed back through the hall to the front door, and a minute later I was running in the rain, thinking what an idiot I was not to have a coat or umbrella or anything. It was too late for that now, though, so I just went as fast as I could, feeling my legs starting to tremble as I plunged into the heavy, folding darkness. It was such a relief to see the outside light on at Pets' Place. I wasn't sure if someone had left it on by mistake or if it was just a light that stayed on all night, but I was glad anyway and I hurried the last few steps to the door and pushed the handle down.

The feeling of disappointment when I realized the door was locked was too much to bear and I was close to tears when I suddenly remembered Mia mentioning the spare key. So I groped my way along the side of the shed until I came to the window, bent down and slid my fingers under a stone. Bingo! I turned the key in the lock and pushed open the door.

"Sorry to disturb you everyone," I said, switching on the light.

It was nice to hear all the scuffling noises. I didn't feel so alone anymore. Buddy thumped his foot when he saw me and I took him out of his hutch and cuddled him. Sometimes he stays still when he's being held, and sometimes he doesn't. Today he was in his floppy nighttime mood, and nuzzled his nose into my neck, which felt nice.

"Do rabbits feel things like humans do, Buddy?" I whispered into his fur. "I mean, do you miss me when I'm not here? I hope not, for your sake. I wish I was you, then I'd only have to worry about eating and sleeping and I wouldn't care about feeling left out of games or friendships."

Buddy felt so warm and soft, that I told him all about Lydia. "She's determined to be best friends with Naomi, Bud, and I can tell she wishes I'd move to the other end of the planet. Well, maybe not to the other end of the planet but I bet she'd like to be in Amethyst dorm instead of me. I'm not going anywhere, though, because I *like* Naomi and she likes me, so that's that." I stroked Buddy's ears. "Nao's a nice nickname, isn't it? Better than *Name* anyway. I wonder if one day someone here might call me Kates, like Mom and Dad do."

I stayed silent for a moment after that, thinking how ridiculous it was talking to a rabbit, but oddly enough, Mom had been right, it was definitely making me feel better. When I finally put Buddy back in his hutch I noticed there were lots of straw pieces sticking to my top. I brushed them off as best I could, then locked up and started rushing back to Hazeldean through the drizzle. The closer I got, the more the lights of the building guided me, but I preferred it when it was darker because now I felt as though I was really on show, so I broke into a run and prayed that no one could see me through a window. I also prayed that the front door wouldn't be locked, because nine o'clock is lock-up time.

What if Miss Carol was waiting to pounce on me in the hall and give me a massive telling-off? I breathed a huge sigh of relief when the front door opened, but my heart was still pounding as I looked around in big fear. No one was in the hall, thank goodness, so I didn't waste a second, just raced up the stairs faster than ever before.

"What time do you call this, young lady?" came Miss Jennings's stern voice from just behind me as I was going into my dorm. "And why are you all wet?"

"Sorry, Miss Jennings. I was looking out of the window and I thought I saw something shiny on the ground, so I went out to get it in case it was important..."

Miss Jennings was frowning hard. "And where is it?"

"It was just a silver chocolate wrapper. I've thrown it away."

She nodded. "Well, it wasn't very sensible, going out in the pouring rain. Go and get ready for bed quickly and if you're this late again you'll have early bed the following night."

"Sorry," I mumbled, hurrying into the dorm.

"Where have you been?" asked Naomi, rushing at me with wide eyes and grabbing my shoulders. "You're all wet."

I suddenly felt stupid saying I'd gone to see Buddy. I'd only have to explain why and that might lead to awkward questions, so I told the same lie I'd just told Miss Jennings and got changed into my jammies at lightning speed at the same time.

"What's this in your hair?" asked Georgie, pulling out a piece of straw. "Are you sure you haven't been to see Buddy Bunnykins?"

I wished then that I'd told the truth in the first place, but I could hardly go back on it now. "You're joking! I'd be too scared in the dark!"

Then I whizzed along to the bathroom, with a picture in my head of Naomi's still face with its anxious, puzzled expression. Had she realized I'd told a lie? No, she couldn't have, could she? Maybe I should tell her the truth the next day. But how could I? There'd be too much explaining to do, like why I was suddenly missing Mom so much and what was making me so worried that I needed to go and talk to Buddy at ten-to-nine at night.

No, it was too late now. I was stuck with the lie.

Chapter Eight

It's funny how things always seem so much better during the day than they do at nighttime. The day after my little talk with Buddy, Naomi was completely bright and breezy and normal, and I told myself that one little white lie wasn't the end of the world. Then two nice things happened. Firstly, I talked to Mam'zelle Clemence about the fashion design club.

"I came to look for you at Oakley but you weren't there," I began.

"Oh dear. I'm sorrrrry you had a wasted journey," she replied, which didn't give me any clues at all about whether Lydia had deliberately sent me on a wild goose chase. "My idea is to link up with one of ze art teachers and form a club together, designing and making jewelry. I'll let you know how zings go, Kateee," she added, "but I'm sure we'll get someseeng off zee ground."

The second good thing was running club, which was great fun. We warmed up in the hall to music, then went down to the track and ran relays. We had to get into pairs and I went with Naomi. Strangely, Lydia didn't seem to mind. She seemed perfectly happy to be Grace's partner. It seemed strange but I was pleased. It would be so great if she'd finally accepted that I was Naomi's friend too.

After running club we all went to get changed and showered. "See you at dinner, everyone," said Lydia, as she went off to Opal. "Save me a place if you get there first."

She grinned at us all and I felt a nice feeling that at last things were looking up.

When Naomi and I went into the dorm after our showers, Grace was on her knees pulling stuff out of her bottom drawer. Her face was white and I could see she was in a state.

"What's the matter?" I asked, crouching down beside her.

"I don't get it…" she said softly. "I just don't get it…"

"What?" Naomi asked, coming over too.

"Before running club I came up here to get my stopwatch but I couldn't find it and there wasn't time to look more, so I thought I'd have a thorough search later. And now I have…and it's not here."

"Where else have you looked?" I asked.

"This is the only place where it could possibly be. I keep all my precious private things in this box right at the back of my drawer."

I caught a glimpse of a red and gold patterned lid, before Grace shut her drawer and sat down heavily, leaning against the wall with her head flopped forward.

Jess came in a moment later and looked horrified when she heard what had happened. "Just think carefully, Grace. Are you certain you didn't take it to running club?"

Grace sighed. "Double positive." She looked at me. "You and Naomi were the last to use it yesterday."

"But we gave it back to you at dinner," I quickly pointed out.

Grace nodded. "I know."

"And are you certain you put it back after that?" asked Jess.

"Well, I *was* certain, but now I'm wondering if I actually did, because it can't just disappear, can it?"

Jess made Grace take one more careful look all through her drawers, in her bed, on her desk. Everywhere. Then we had to go to dinner.

"We'll report it to Miss Carol," said Naomi. "She can give out a notice in assembly, then everyone'll be looking for it."

"If we skip dessert we'll have time to go to the changing room and look for it before study hour," I added.

Naomi nodded. "How about *you* look in the changing room, Jess, and Katy and I go down the field."

"I'll look on the ground between the cafeteria and Hazeldean," said Grace, looking really glum. "I can't imagine that I dropped it though. I always keep it deep in my pocket."

Georgie, Mia and Lydia heard about the missing stopwatch at dinner and offered to help with the search. So as soon as we'd wolfed down our lemon chicken we all raced off. Lydia searched the changing-room area. Naomi said she didn't think there was much point in going down to the athletics field after all because we knew perfectly well we'd given the stopwatch back to Grace, so in the end she and I went into Hazeldean and looked absolutely everywhere.

We were all very subdued during study hour because Grace was nearly in tears. "I can easily get another stopwatch," she said, "it's just that this one is really precious."

Jess put her arm around Grace. "I'm sure it'll turn up somewhere," she said. "It didn't just disappear."

"Unless someone's taken it," said Grace quietly.

"No one would do that, surely," said Lydia, and we all agreed, but I had to admit I was getting anxious in case that was what had happened. There just didn't seem to be any other answer.

After study hour I had a nice surprise because Mom called me when we were on our way to tell Miss Carol what had happened.

"See you in the common room," I said, hanging back to talk with Mom. And of course the first thing I told her about was Grace's stopwatch going missing.

"Poor girl," said Mom. "Have the dorm parents been notified?"

"The others have gone to tell Miss Carol right now. Do you think someone might have taken it, Mom?"

"Well someone might have found it and decided

to keep it, not realizing how precious it is to Grace."

After that we talked about *The Fast Lane,* and Mom told me how one of the actors was having a baby in real life so they were having to let her character be pregnant too. Then I told Mom about Naomi's secret being out, which led to a long conversation about my own secret and how relieved I was that I'd managed to keep it so far.

The following morning it was whole-school assembly and the Amethyst girls were extra quiet when it came to the announcements at the end.

"I have something particularly important to report this morning, girls," Ms. Carmichael began, in her slow careful voice that always reminded me of a world leader speaking. "One of the girls from Hazeldean boarding house has lost a precious possession. It's a silver stopwatch with all sorts of functions on it, so it is valuable in itself." She paused. "But it has a greater value too. It was a present from this girl's great-grandmother who has now died."

There was a silence after those words. Grace wasn't next to me so I couldn't tell how she was feeling. No one moved a muscle as we waited to hear what was coming next.

"It may be that one of you has come across the stopwatch and not realized its value, in which case you might now be regretting having taken it. If this is the case then all the teachers would be sympathetic. You simply have to hand the stopwatch in and it will be returned to its owner and nothing more will be said."

Ms. Carmichael's eyes seemed to tour around everyone and we held our breath because it was obvious she hadn't finished. When she spoke next, her voice was much quieter and the words came out faster. "However, if the stopwatch has not been returned by the end of the day, I shall have no choice but to ask the dorm parents to search the dorms."

There wasn't a sound and yet it was as though the whole school had done an enormous gasp. We have to stay silent until we're out of the hall, but the moment we spilled into the corridor the words came tumbling out as everyone buzzed with conversation about what Ms. Carmichael had just said.

"Do you know whose stopwatch it is?" I heard lots of people asking.

And others were saying that having our dorms searched was like living in a prison.

"You'll definitely get it back now, Grace!" hissed Georgie the moment we were on our own.

"Yes, I don't think anyone's going to search our dorms," said Naomi. "It's just a good way of scaring the person who's taken it."

"Really?" said Lydia. "You think Ms. Carmichael was just saying that?"

"Yes, I agree with Naomi," said Jess. "It's pretty clever, isn't it, Grace?"

Grace didn't look convinced. "If someone really wanted to keep it they could hide it somewhere else."

"Well, let's wait and see what happens today," said Mia. And we all agreed that we'd go back to Hazeldean at morning break to see if there was any news.

Miss Carol was busy on the phone and didn't look too thrilled to see us. "I can understand that you're anxious," she said, when she'd put the phone down a little impatiently, "but you really need to concentrate on your schoolwork." She put her hand on Grace's shoulder. "As soon as there is any news I'll be the first to hear about it and I'll come and find you, Grace."

So after lunch, even though we were all dying to go back over to Hazeldean, Grace said it was pointless. "I'm going down to the athletics field. Anyone coming?"

"I'm going for a walk," said Naomi. "Save me a place in history, yeah?"

"Where are you going?" asked Lydia.

"Just around," said Naomi.

And Lydia didn't insist on going with her, thank goodness. Maybe she'd finally realized that, princess or not, sometimes Naomi simply liked being alone.

"Coming to feed the pets?" Mia asked me.

Georgie rolled her eyes and said she'd put up with the stinky animal smell and come along too as she didn't have anything better to do. Then Lydia surprised me by saying she'd like to see Buddy and the guinea pigs.

"I used to have pets when I was little but I grew out of them when I was about eight," she told us, as Mia got Porgy and Bess out of their hutch.

"Do you want to hold them, Lydia?"

"No thanks. Let's see Buddy."

"I'm going to put him in his run. That's where he grazes," I explained as I lifted Buddy out. But Lydia didn't seem interested. She was bending over, poking around at the back of his hutch.

"What are you doing?" asked Georgie. "You'll get poop on your hand, you know!"

Then her words froze in the air because Lydia was standing up straight, and on her outstretched palm lay Grace's stopwatch. My body jolted as though I'd had an electric shock as we all stared at the stopwatch in horror, and my face went white as I felt everyone's eyes on me.

"What's this doing in Buddy's hutch?" Lydia asked me quietly.

I looked at her and in that split second I saw a fleeting look of triumph on her face and guessed exactly what had happened. She'd planted it in the hutch. Lydia had actually sunk so low as to take the stopwatch and make it look as though *I'd* taken it. But how could I say that? Why should anyone believe me? I was trapped. Completely trapped. It was as though the ceiling was caving in. I could hardly breathe. I had to get out.

I thrust Buddy back in his hutch, pushed past Lydia and hurled myself out of Pets' Place. Then I ran toward the athletics track but went straight past it, catching a glimpse of Grace on the way. Tears were streaming down my face, but I kept running and running across the pathway between some trees and along the edge of another field. I was probably off school grounds but I didn't care, and then suddenly I came upon a high hedge and plunged through a narrow archway to find myself in a garden.

"Katy! What's wrong? What's happened?"

I gasped. It was Naomi. She was sitting on a little bench. This must be the secret place she'd been going to show me two days before. The place where she came to get away from everyone. And I'd interrupted her peace.

"I..." But I couldn't speak because of crying. I turned to go and she came after me, turned me around and steered me back toward the bench. I sat down beside her and buried my face in my hands. Her arm went around me and she patted my shoulder and said some words that must have been Ghanaian.

"Sorry," I managed to say, pulling away from her and trying to stop crying. "Do you have a tissue?" She didn't, so I used my sleeve to wipe my tears, and she kept encouraging me to tell her what had happened.

In the end I just blurted out, "Grace's stopwatch has turned up—"

"But that's great!" Naomi interrupted. "Where?"

"In Buddy's hutch."

There was a silence.

"I don't expect you to believe me, Naomi, but I swear I have no idea how it got there. Well...actually I *do* have some idea."

Another silence. I was staring at the ground so I couldn't see Naomi's expression, but I could imagine the puzzled look on her face. "How?" she asked eventually.

I took a deep breath. "I think...Lydia planted it there."

Naomi gasped. "But...why would she do that?"

"Because she doesn't like me being friends with you. She's jealous of me." My words were tumbling out, but even as I was saying them I realized they sounded stupid and pathetic. "She wants you for herself. I sometimes think she really hates me...the way she's always putting me down and saying I'm immature and everything. You don't see it, Naomi, because she's always nice with you... But she's so stuck-up and she looks down on me..."

Another silence. This was awful. Then Naomi bit her lip. "However...stuck-up she is, I'm sure she'd never do anything as bad as taking Grace's most treasured possession and planting it on someone, Katy. Do you have any proof...or is it just that you think she's jealous?"

"Well…no…but…" I looked straight at Naomi for the first time. "You do believe that I didn't take it, don't you?"

"I can't imagine you doing anything like that. Not in a million years."

"Thank goodness for that, because I'm scared the others aren't going to believe me…"

"Well, what exactly happened? Tell me the whole story, Katy."

So I did, starting from Mia saying she was going to feed the pets and the others all coming too, and finishing with me running out of Pets' Place in tears. Naomi didn't interrupt me all the way through and at the end she just shook her head sadly and said, "Poor you." Then she looked at her watch and jumped to her feet. "Oh no, the bell must have gone ages ago. We'd better get back."

"I can't go to class as though nothing has happened," I said, feeling panic rising up in me. "No one'll talk to me. The whole school will probably think I'm a horrible thief by now…"

"Don't worry. Mia will have told Grace and Grace will have told Miss Carol…"

"And Miss Carol is probably waiting until *I* turn up so she can tell me what a terrible person I am and keep me in detention every day until Christmas."

"No she won't. She'd never do anything like that. But you'd better go and see her right away. I'll go to class, then I can tell the others that you're safe."

"They won't care. They'll all hate me," I said. "Lydia will have made sure of that. And there's nothing I can do. No way I can prove I'm innocent." I sat back down heavily. "It's so unfair."

Naomi closed her eyes and then opened them very slowly. "All I can say is that my father is a very wise man and I always remember something he said to me when I was eight and I'd told a lie and thought I could get away with it. He said, 'The truth is the best tool of all, so if it goes missing, don't make do with any other tool, just wait for the truth to turn up.'"

I was in too much of a state to think about what those words really meant. I just started stumbling back toward school as Naomi ran on ahead of me.

"I'll tell the history teacher you're not well. And I'll make sure the others realize that just because the stopwatch was found in Buddy's cage it doesn't prove anything."

I nodded and watched Naomi rushing off, then two seconds later she came back and gave me a big hug. "Don't tell anyone about this garden, will you? It's my secret place – where I come to be on my own when I get fed up with...the world."

I shook my head.

"Go and see Miss Carol, will you? She'll tell you what to do."

Then she was gone again and I was left to plod my way slowly back, going over all that Naomi had said. I started by thinking about the moment when I'd asked her straight out if she believed me and she'd said, *"I can't imagine you doing anything like that. Not in a million years."* At least that was one good thing. I wouldn't be able to bear it if Naomi didn't believe me. But then I frowned and stopped walking as I realized with a jolt that she hadn't actually said she believed me. She'd just said she couldn't imagine me doing anything like that. Was that the same? I wasn't sure. All I knew was that I wished I could wake up and find the whole thing had been a terrible nightmare.

Miss Carol answered the door to her apartment as soon as I knocked. She looked serious but not angry. "Come in," she said. "Grace has been to see me with one or two of the others. I understand the stopwatch was found in your rabbit's cage."

I nodded but couldn't speak.

"Sit down, Katy, and try to tell me what happened."

I sighed as I sat down and really had to force myself to speak. "I didn't put it there. I don't know how it got there. I'd never steal anything from anyone."

Miss Carol's eyebrows nearly joined up when she frowned. I found myself staring at them, and then had to quickly look away in case she thought I was being rude.

"If you didn't put it there yourself, do you have any idea who might have?"

I was just about to say Lydia's name when I stopped myself. What was the point? I had no proof that Lydia could have done it. And if I tried to explain what she was like, it would sound stupid. So I just shook my head miserably, then asked her what was going to happen to me.

"Nobody's blaming you, Katy. Grace is naturally very upset but I've asked her to try and be open-minded until we get to the bottom of this."

"What about Mia and Georgie? Did they come to see you too?"

"Yes, and Lydia."

I tried not to let anything show on my face. "And what did they say?"

"They mentioned that you ran off in tears..."

"I felt trapped. I had to get out."

"They didn't understand why you didn't defend yourself. I think they felt a little suspicious about that."

"Yes, but how could I? I've got no proof." Suddenly I felt furious. This whole thing was so unfair. I stood up and shouted at Miss Carol. "Nobody believes me! It doesn't make any difference, does it? You can hate me, same as everyone else, because no one can ever find out the truth because I can't prove it!"

Then I burst into tears all over again and Miss Carol gave me a handful of tissues and tried to hold my hand, but I pulled away.

"Listen, Katy, no one's going to hate you, because no one is going to find out. I told Grace and the others who came to see me that they must keep completely quiet about the whole thing. And if it comes to my notice that Lydia or anyone from Amethyst has been talking about the matter, they will be in serious trouble."

"That'll make them hate me even more. And what about me? What's going to happen?"

"If you can put your hand on your heart and say that you have no idea how that stopwatch got in your rabbit's cage, and nothing more comes to light, then I will draw a line across the whole thing and it will be forgotten. A notice will go out telling everyone that the stopwatch has turned up, and that will be the end of the matter. You'd be amazed how quickly things blow over at Silver Spires. Believe me, in a couple of days' time no one will give it another thought."

"Except my friends..." I said quietly. "They'll always wonder."

"Not if they're true friends," said Miss Carol.

I missed history altogether and met the others outside. Jess, Georgie and Mia went on ahead and my heart started beating so hard I thought it would burst out of my body. Grace didn't look at me at all. Neither did Lydia, but Naomi gave me a nice smile. All I wanted was to get afternoon school over with so I could go and call Mom. I'd already decided to tell Mrs. Mellor I wasn't feeling well because I couldn't face running club.

But in the end I couldn't get through to Mom, so I sat at my desk playing CDs and covering pages and pages of my sketchbook with patterns for material. I love trying out different colors together and right now it was the only thing that could help to calm me down. Those words of Naomi's father's, about the truth going missing and how you had to wait for it to turn up, kept on going through my head. But what was the point of waiting? Even if I accused

Lydia straight out of planting the stopwatch on me, she'd just deny that she knew anything about it. So how could the truth *ever* turn up?

I was on the next-to-last page of my sketchbook when Georgie came crashing in. "I went to modern dance. It just about killed me but I'm not giving it up because the teacher says you need dance skills to be an actress."

I was totally shocked but really pleased that she was acting completely normally, and I was on the verge of saying something about being sorry I'd run off in tears, when she kept going. "Miss Carol says we're not allowed to talk about '*it*', by the way, and the others are all really upset with you, but I believe you." She lowered her voice. "And I've got a pretty good idea who put that stopwatch in Buddy's cage." She mouthed the word "Lydia," and added, "I went and told Miss Carol that too, but she said I couldn't go around accusing people of doing things without an atom of proof."

I could have hugged Georgie. "And what's Lydia been saying herself?"

"Dunno. I'm keeping out of her way." Georgie looked over my shoulder at the pattern I'd done. "Nice. Are you coming to study hour, by the way?"

"Yes, course." And as I got my books together

I sighed to myself and wondered if Naomi's father had a plan for what to do if the truth was not just missing, but lost for good.

Chapter Nine

The next two days were horrible because out of my group of friends, only Georgie and Naomi spoke to me, and as far as Georgie was concerned, never when anyone else was around. The others were cool and distant, and Lydia tossed her head and looked in the other direction the moment I appeared. I was totally miserable and wished I could skip the next ten days and go home to Dad early. But I wouldn't be able to enjoy it because of the thought of coming back to Silver Spires hanging over me all the time. It would be best if I could just leave Silver Spires and never come back.

But eventually Miss Carol was proven right. After a while people seemed to forget about the whole stopwatch episode and things started to go back to normal, just like she'd said they would. Nobody discussed it around school anymore, and Mia and Jess started talking to me again. Then Grace did too. I can't say they were exactly the friendliest people in the whole world, but at least they were talking. I wished it was because they believed me, though, and not just out of habit.

Naomi didn't act any differently from how she'd acted ever since we'd spoken in the garden, and that was the saddest thing of all, because our friendship seemed to have disappeared for good. We didn't laugh together anymore or have fun. I didn't feel close to her like I used to. Although she was always perfectly nice to me, we'd lost our bond and that made me really depressed and a little afraid. I would see her joking around with Lydia, but it was as though I was looking at the two of them through a camera lens that was out of focus. It didn't seem real somehow. And I'd think bitterly to myself that Lydia had gotten her way. This was exactly what she'd wanted to happen. Then once or twice I noticed a sad look on Naomi's face and wondered if she was still thinking about all that had happened and puzzling over why the truth hadn't come out yet.

One lunchtime, we were putting our trays away when she said she had something to ask me. We walked toward Hazeldean and eventually she spoke.

"You know that night when you went out in the rain and you were late for bed?"

"Yes..."

"And you know you had straw in your hair?"

I started to feel sick. "Yes."

"And you know how Georgie asked if you'd been to see Buddy, and you said you hadn't?"

The panic I felt was breaking out in an argument inside my head. It was *me* against *me*.

Don't say you were anywhere near Buddy that night, or she'll definitely think you stole the stopwatch.

But I can't lie to Naomi.

You'll have to. The truth will only make matters worse.

No, the truth is important – the best tool of all, remember?

But...

Just explain. Go on! NOW!

"This is going to sound terrible," I began in a small voice, "but I was upset about something to do with Mom and I couldn't tell anyone...except Buddy."

I managed to meet her eyes and all I could see was

doubt. Deep, deep layers of doubt. She didn't believe me. And suddenly I couldn't bear the unfairness of it all and I saw red. "Just tell me, Naomi," I said in a horrible voice, "exactly *why* would I want to steal Grace's stopwatch? What possible reason would I have for doing that?"

She looked shocked. "Yes, I know. I kept saying that to myself but then I remembered the straw in your hair and...well, what am I supposed to think?"

I knew my voice was getting louder but I couldn't help it. "Don't you think that Lydia has every reason under the sun to steal the stopwatch and then pin the blame on me? You *know* she doesn't want you to like me. She wants you all for herself. I don't get why you can't just see that, Naomi."

And that's when I realized Lydia was right behind us. "Katy Parsons! You are such a sneaky little thief. You've had it in for me ever since I arrived at this place. But you're the one who borrowed that stopwatch! You're the one who loved it so much you wanted one for Christmas! The problem is *you* can't accept that Naomi might actually want to be friends with someone other than you, and now you're accusing me of taking Grace's stopwatch? But I wouldn't even know where to take it from.

I don't know where Grace keeps her stuff. You make me sick!"

She raced off and Naomi instantly went after her, so I was left standing there feeling like an idiot and wishing I'd not lost my temper in front of Naomi, because now everything was ten times worse than before. I heaved a sad sigh and knew I had to talk to Mom right now, because this was unbearable. I tapped in her number, then listened to it ring six times before the voicemail message came on.

"Hi, this is Cally's phone. Leave me a message and I'll get back to you."

I disconnected and let my cell phone drop to my side. Everything seemed worse than ever now. Then I suddenly felt sick as I realized another bad thing. Mom hadn't texted or called or e-mailed for three days. Why was that? I knew it was silly, but instantly my mind went to the stopwatch. Had Miss Carol called her and told her what had happened? Was Mom so upset that she couldn't even bear to talk to me?

I told myself to stop being so stupid and irrational. Of course Miss Carol wouldn't tell Mom when there was no proof that I'd done anything wrong. And even if she *had* told her, Mom would have been in touch right away, wouldn't she? But she hadn't been

138

in touch, had she? And then I was back in the middle of my anxiety again because I simply couldn't think of any other explanation. Mom had never left it for three days without calling before.

I tapped in her number again and this time when the voicemail message came on I spoke in a shaky voice. *"Hi, Mom, it's me. If you've heard from Miss Carol I absolutely swear it's not true. And I...love you lots."*

All afternoon I felt miserable. Georgie and Mia wanted to know if anything had happened, but I didn't dare to try and explain what Naomi had said to me about the straw in my hair because that would probably get me into even deeper trouble. I just said I was sad because I hadn't heard from Mom in awhile.

I kept my phone on silent during study hour, even though they're supposed to be switched off, and used up all my concentration on willing it to ring, which meant I didn't get much geography done. The teacher wouldn't be too pleased, but I didn't care about that because I had much bigger things on my mind.

It was a relief to go up to the dorm and get my sketchbook out, though I didn't know what to draw now. Nothing could inspire me today. It wasn't bedtime for another half-hour but no one seemed to be in the mood for going to the common room. We were all lying on our beds or sitting at our desks, and, as usual these days, Lydia was sitting cross-legged on the big rug with Naomi. It was almost fall break, and what was it Miss Carol said to Lydia on that very first day here? *We stick with the same dorm mates for the first half of the semester...* I bet Lydia was thinking, *Only two more days to go before I can ask Miss Carol if I can switch dorms with Katy.* Maybe Naomi and Lydia had already been to see Miss Carol. I'd been doodling on the front cover of my sketchbook while I'd been having these thoughts, and when I looked at the doodle I realized it looked like heavy drops of rain falling into a flat pond.

Lydia was leafing through a magazine and looking very excited about something or other.

"We never did have our midnight feast, did we? Let's do it tomorrow, hey?" she said, looking around at everyone except me. "We can all smuggle stuff out of breakfast, lunch and dinner, and have a feast! I'll sneak out of my dorm and come up here. No probs."

Surprisingly, no one was particularly enthusiastic. We were all floppy and tired. I sighed as I opened my sketchbook and leafed through the pages of designs. The fashion club hadn't gotten off the ground yet because Mr. Cary, the art teacher who was supposed to be joining up with Mam'zelle Clemence, was ill, and since the discovery of the stopwatch I hadn't felt like drawing. But I knew I couldn't stay in a depressed mood all the time. I had to snap out of it and get on with some jewelry designs. Then, as soon as the art teacher was better and the club was set up I'd be able to start creating my designs.

"What are you designing now, Katy?" asked Georgie, peering down from her bed.

"Earrings."

"Cool! Can you design some for me? Something really crazy!"

"Or something simple and silver for me," said Naomi.

"*Or* something little and boring for me," said Mia, wrinkling her nose.

"You're not little and boring, Mia," protested Georgie. "You're little and sweet! But, tell you what, Katy, if you really want a challenge, try designing something for Grace. I mean, something that she'd actually agree to wear!"

"What a thing to say!" said Grace, pretending to be hurt.

It was so nice to hear them all talking normally to me. I looked carefully at Grace's face before turning to the last clean page. Inspiration came flooding in and I felt a moment of happiness after being miserable for so long. "Okay, Grace, I'm going to design you the perfect pair."

"Yes, and when Mam'zelle Clemence finally starts her fashion club, you can actually make them," said Jess.

"But my ears aren't even pierced!" said Grace. "You ought to choose someone else, Katy. I'm just not into jewelry at all."

"Yes, you are!" Lydia chimed in. "What about that little charm bracelet you've got..."

There was a silence, but I didn't realize anything was wrong until I looked up from my sketchbook and saw that Grace's face was pale and she was staring at Lydia as though she'd turned into a monster.

"What?" said Jess, sitting up sharply. "What's wrong, Grace?"

I'd never heard Grace's voice sound so fragile as it did just then. "How did you know about that bracelet, Lydia?"

The silence was like thin thin glass. Nobody moved. Nobody wanted to step on the glass.

"I...I've just seen it, that's all," said Lydia, trying to sound casual, but it was obvious she was unsure

142

of herself because she was flipping over the pages of her magazine at top speed and her eyes weren't focusing on anything.

Grace seemed to be having trouble speaking. Her voice was shaking. "It's impossible to just *see* it, Lydia. Nobody's ever seen it because I keep it in my special box at the back of my bottom drawer with my other precious things..."

Lydia's face flooded with color and she slapped her magazine shut with a loud huff of annoyance.

Then we all gasped as Grace finished her sentence. "...like my stopwatch."

The words rang around the dorm as Lydia got up with a face like fury, which she turned on me. "All right, Little Miss Fashion, you don't have to stare at me like that, you know. You *made* me do it, always trying to push me out and keep Naomi to yourself. Well, I don't care. There are loads of people who want to be my friend and, unlike some people, I'm not impressed by princesses so you can stuff yourself."

And with that she left the room. No pushing past people. No floods of tears. Completely calmly, her head held high.

The door clicked shut and the rest of us were left in stunned silence, but it wasn't like glass anymore, it was liquid and flowing, swirling around, buoying me up. I didn't have to worry now. The missing truth had turned up. One by one I met the eyes of my friends as the silence slowly dissolved and the world came back into focus.

"I knew it!" said Georgie, eyes wide. Then she repeated it slowly as though those were the only words she could manage. "I! KNEW! IT!"

Jess just looked shocked, but Mia leaned her head against mine. "Georgie was right."

"It must have been awful, Katy," whispered Grace.

And Naomi looked as if she was going to cry as she put her arms around me and gave me a tight hug. I felt like crying myself then, but not out of sadness – out of big big relief.

"Pretty wise dad I've got," said Naomi, pulling out of the hug and smiling at me with tears in her eyes. "What do you think, Katy?"

I grinned back and we high-fived each other. "You're not kidding!"

Then everyone wanted to know what we were talking about, so I had to explain about running into Naomi when I was crying my eyes out and how she'd tried to make me feel better. And Georgie wanted to go through absolutely everything that had happened, and kept saying, "I can't believe that girl! I just can't believe her!" And I got hugs and more hugs and sympathetic words that lifted me up and up, until by the time it was bedtime I was on top of the world.

Chapter Ten

The next day Naomi and I were inseparable. It was a little embarrassing seeing Lydia at breakfast and in classes, but the weird thing was that Lydia herself didn't seem at all embarrassed. She'd been right when she'd said that lots of people wanted to be her friend, because every time we came across her she was talking and laughing with someone or other. She was probably telling them how famous she was in Europe.

After lunch, Naomi and I walked across to Oakley to find out from Mam'zelle Clemence if Mr. Cary was back yet. I felt so close to Naomi just then that

I suddenly had the urge to tell her my secret. After all, we were in exactly the same boat and I knew she'd never ever tell a soul. But just when I was on the verge of speaking, we came across a group of older girls coming out of Oakley, and I knew I'd have to wait for another time to share my secret. There was sure to be a perfect moment.

The girls saw Naomi and broke into smiles. "Whoooo, we're very honored!" one of them said. "A royal visit!"

She wasn't being sarcastic, just joking around, but Naomi looked down and I could tell she was upset.

"Don't listen to Emma!" said another of the girls. "She's only teasing."

The girl named Emma suddenly turned serious. "Yeah, sorry, Naomi. You must get fed up with people talking about it all the time and wanting to get in on your interviews and everything."

"What?!"

Naomi and I had both spoken together but it was Naomi who continued while I stood there, open-mouthed. "How did you know I did an interview?"

The girl looked surprised. "Sorry, I didn't know it was a secret... I had to deliver a note from Mam'zelle Clemence to Miss Carol one Saturday, and the door to Miss Carol's apartment was open. I went in, but then I could hear that she was busy in the kitchen, so I just crept in and left the note on her table. She had visitors and I heard one of them saying that a passing student had just mentioned that she was Naomi's best friend. Then I heard the other one say, 'Amazing, isn't it, how everyone wants to be best friends with a princess? She probably hoped she'd get in on the interview!' And that's how I found out."

Emma shrugged. "Anyway, see ya!" And off they went, leaving the two of us standing there in a state of shock.

Naomi was the first to speak. "So it was Lydia's fault again. I should have realized, shouldn't I? I mean she started acting like my best friend before she even knew me."

"And she acted like she knew exactly what it was like to be a princess, didn't she? I mean she never asked you any questions or anything. She wasn't really interested in who you are at all."

Naomi giggled. "Not like Georgie… Do you remember? On the way up to the dorm when I first got here?"

"Good old Georgie!" I laughed. "It's just the way she is!"

"I know," smiled Naomi. "And you, Kates," she went on. "You were great...almost as though you really knew what it was like..."

And suddenly there it was. The perfect moment.

"I do."

"Do what?

"Know what it's like. I'm kind of...in the same boat, you see..."

There. I'd said it. But I wasn't upset with myself. I just felt completely calm. I trusted Naomi. She was my best friend.

"In...the same...boat?"

I spoke quietly. "You know I said I went to see Buddy because I was upset about something to do with Mom?"

"Yes."

"Well, it was because I'd just seen her on Lydia's DVD and I suddenly missed her. You see...my mother is Cally Jamieson."

Naomi gasped, then looked at me with big eyes and mouthed the words, "Cally...Jamieson..." in slow motion.

But only a second later her shock seemed to melt away and she was instantly back to her calm self. "Sorry, that's probably the very reaction you *don't* want!"

"Thank goodness for that. I thought you'd lost the power of speech!"

There was a pause, then Naomi spluttered and we both cracked up laughing because it suddenly seemed such a ridiculous moment. I recovered first.

"You won't tell anyone, will you?"

"You *know* I won't." She put her hand on her heart. "I swear on best friendship."

Then Mam'zelle Clemence's voice brought us back to the here and now. She was rushing out of Oakley, heading toward the main building.

"Katy! Good news. Mr. Cary is better so zee club can start after zee holidays, yes?"

"Oh yes, that's great!" I agreed as she went by like a whirlwind.

"Look!" said Naomi. "There's Grace and the others. They look like they're up to something!"

Typically it was Grace who caught up to us first and she wasn't even out of breath. "I've just told Miss Carol the whole story," she gabbled. "And she said she'd deal with Lydia herself and that we should just leave it alone now..."

"Yes," said Mia, rushing up, "and Miss Carol said that she's really proud of Amethyst dorm, especially you, Katy."

"And she said we shouldn't be too hard on Lydia,"

said Jess, "because she's probably just been homesick, as it affects everyone in different ways and especially if you're an only child!"

"But she said she had a big family!" I spluttered.

"And there's more," said Georgie, puffing her way up to us. "Let me tell them this part, guys."

The others kept quiet and waited.

Georgie grinned around at us, loving being the center of attention. "And Miss Carol just *happened* to mention that Lydia's parents only live about thirty miles away!"

"After all that about living in London!" added Mia.

Naomi winked at me, then turned to Georgie. "Well we can top that…"

And as we all walked back to the main building, we told the others what Emma had said.

"Incredible!" said Jess, turning to Naomi. "So, okay, she didn't do it on purpose, but it was actually Lydia's fault that your secret was leaked!" Then Jess must have remembered why Naomi and I had been going to Oakley in the first place. "Did you find out about the fashion club, Katy?"

"Yes and it's…" But my phone had starting ringing so I pulled it out of my pocket, glanced at the screen, then pressed the green button ecstatically. "Mom!"

I was only vaguely aware of the others laughing in the background because I was so tuned in to what Mom was saying.

"Oh, Kates! It's wonderful to hear your voice. My phone was stolen – at least that's what I thought, only it turned up in some grass where we've been filming an episode with a baseball game in it – and I've been going nuts wondering what to do because filming has been so intensive, and then when one of the crew found my phone it was totally wonderful!"

"It's okay, Mom. I've just been panicking that you were upset with me... Did you get my message?"

"No, I haven't even listened to my messages yet because the moment my phone turned up I wanted to call you right away. I'm supposed to be on set right now actually, but they can wait."

"Well don't worry... When you pick up the message just ignore it because it turns out that a girl named Lydia took Grace's stopwatch and planted it on me because she wanted Naomi to stop liking me, but it's all sorted out now and the Amethyst team knows the truth."

Mom laughed. "Sounds like something we could use in a *Fast Lane* plot! But I'm glad it's all sorted out, honey, it must have been horrible... You'll have to tell me all about it in detail when—"

"Yes, I'll e-mail you the whole story."

"I was going to say you can tell me when I see you this weekend."

I gasped, and all my friends must have realized that Mom had said something incredible, because I was aware of them suddenly standing like statues around me.

"What do you mean, this weekend, Mom?"

"I'm flying home, Kates. I wanted to be there for you during your break."

"That's the best news ever! I can't wait! I can tell you all about absolutely everything!"

Mom laughed. "I can't wait either. Save it all up, honey and I'll see you very soon!"

So I hung up and looked straight at Naomi, bursting to tell her my wonderful news. "Mom's flying back so I'll see her at fall break!"

Naomi grabbed both my hands and we did a crazy dance around and around, with me whooping for joy. "What a great surprise, Kates!" But the bell for afternoon classes broke into our happiness.

"So where's your mom flying back from?" Georgie wanted to know.

And that's when I suddenly realized I'd forgotten all about my secret for a moment there. At lightning speed, I ran through my side of the phone conversation to make sure I hadn't given anything away, then just said, "Los Angeles. Remember, she works over there."

"Oh yeah, she's a styler, isn't she?" said Georgie.

"Stylist!" everyone corrected her.

And suddenly I didn't like the lie anymore. These were my friends, we were a team. I knew Naomi the best, and probably Jess the least, but I could trust them all. There wasn't time right now, but I knew in my heart that sometime soon I'd tell them my secret. And I also knew they'd guard it with their lives, because of who they are...

Mia the Musician
Grace the Sportswoman
Georgie the Actress
Jess the Artist
Naomi the Wise One

My true friends.

❋ Turn the page for some
School Friends fun from Katy!

School Friends Fun!

So now you've met me and all my friends at Silver Spires, why not have a "dorm party" with your own friends? There's nothing better than a good girly sleepover, and I've got some great ideas to make it even more fun – and you'll get a fabulous new look into the bargain!

How to hold a fashion party

It's always cool having something new to wear – and it's even better when it's something fabulous and original that you've created yourself! It's not as hard as you might think. Just set the party scene with some great music, and plenty of drinks and snacks, then get your friends together and try out these ideas...

★ Give each other makeovers! Put everyone's clothes and accessories in a big pile and let your friends put an outfit together for you. Don't be afraid to try something new. Even if it's something you never would have chosen yourself, just try it – you might like it!

★ Customize your own T-shirts!
Add some buttons, feathers, ribbon, patches or sequins...you could even go nuts with fabric paint. (Just make sure you ask your parents first!) The only other things you'll need are a needle and thread, or some fabric glue. Hit the stores for more ideas, and unleash the designer in you. And the best part is that you'll never see anyone wearing the same top as yours!

★ Make friendship bracelets – it's really easy! All you need is some colored embroidery thread from a craft store. You can find instructions for different patterns online, or even create your own. You and your friends could all make matching bracelets to show you're a team like us! Or maybe you could make a special personalized bracelet to give to your very best friend.

So what are you waiting for? Grab your friends and have some School Friends fun!

Katy
x

Now turn the page

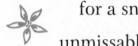

for a sneak preview of the next

unmissable *School Friends* story...

Drama
at
Silver
Spires

Chapter One

I was staring into the distance with a massive smile on my face, imagining myself on a stage somewhere on Broadway. The sound of applause was ringing around the auditorium, and I felt the waves of adoration rolling over me as I took yet another bow. But then this totally cool daydream was interrupted by the sound of my best friend, Mia, whispering my name urgently and tapping me on the leg.

"Georgie!"

I came back to earth with an ugly thud, realizing I wasn't on a stage at all. I was in my school assembly and the principal, Ms. Carmichael, was saying the prayer while every single one of the 360 girls in the hall was bowing her head respectfully. Well, every one except me. I quickly looked down and tried to get myself back into the daydream but got distracted by the sight of a run in my tights. It definitely hadn't been there first thing this morning. I know that for a fact, because Miss Jennings would have spotted it with her eagle eye and made me go back to the dorm to change into a new pair of tights immediately.

Good old Miss Jennings. She's the dorm supervisor at Hazeldean, which is my boarding house at Silver Spires school. Most people find her really strict, and it's true that she keeps her face straight the whole time, which Mia says is totally scary, but personally I like her. The secret is to chit-chat with her lots and tell her jokes and then you can get a smile out of her. Well, *I* can anyway.

Yes I *can*! That makes two things I'm talented at. Acting and getting a smile out of Miss Jennings. Hallelujah! I tell you, it's tough being in a dorm with five other girls who are all completely gorgeous and talented. I mean, take Mia. She came to Silver Spires on a music scholarship because she's so wonderful at piano. Then there's Grace – she got a sports scholarship. As for Jess, she'd definitely have an art scholarship if there *was* such a thing. And

Katy...well she's the trendiest babe on this planet – I'd love to look like Katy – and we all just know she'll finish up as a fashion designer because her sketches are amazing and she's obsessed with the whole fashion scene. And finally – and this is the big one – there's Naomi, who is an African princess. She's also extremely beautiful and very wise. It's just not fair that *all* of them are talented. I mean, how am I supposed to compete with that bunch? They're all my friends and I love them to death, but I sometimes wish they weren't quite so impressive.

Seriously, the only thing I'm good at is acting. Drama has always been my passion. Even when I was only two and a half I used to love dressing up and stuff. My mom said I would stand in the middle of the circle of mothers at play group, wearing an apron from the dress-up box, and entertain everyone by pretending to scrub the floor. Thinking about it, I wonder if I might have developed a bit of a Cinderella obsession, but I don't see how I could have understood the story if I was only two and a half. Aha! Maybe I really am a very smart person but nobody has managed to bring it out of me yet.

"Amen."

Whoops! I think I must have been in another daydream. Anyway, now Ms. Carmichael had finished the prayer we only had the teachers' announcements to go, or notices, as everyone calls them. I wonder why they're called notices when they're not written down. And I also wonder if anyone ever listens to them. I looked around and wasn't surprised to see that most people seemed to have glazed over. Assemblies are probably the most boring part of boarding-school life. Oh and science, and geography… and history. Actually, I can't say I'm a big fan of any classes except drama. The drama class and drama club are the biggest highlights of my week, well, apart from watching *The Fast Lane* on TV, which is my fave show ever. Drama even beats eating smuggled cookies after lights out and stifling giggles with my friends in case Miss Carol, the dorm mom, hears, or going shopping at the beginning of school before you've spent all your allowance. Now, come to think about it, there are hundreds of highlights to boarding-school life – well, to Silver Spires life anyway. Silver Spires is the best school in the world, in case I didn't mention that.

"Georgie!"

Mia was bashing my leg again, but this time when she said my name it didn't sound like a telling-off. In fact for some reason or other Mia was pretty excited. I tuned into what was happening and realized that Miss Pritchard, the senior drama teacher, was standing up. It's funny because the hall was already silent but it went into an even deeper silence when Miss Pritchard began to speak. And personally I went into ecstasy.

"Some of you will know that the junior play will be staged before Christmas break. Anyone in sixth, seventh or eighth grade can audition. The play is called *Castles in the Air* and it's based on the book *Little Women* by Louisa M. Alcott."

My heart hammered with excitement. A play. How fantastic is that? And *Little Women* is my favorite book ever.

"I'm sure many of you have read the book," went on Miss Pritchard, "and know that the story is centered around four sisters: Meg, Jo, Beth and Amy."

Just hearing those four names felt magical, especially the name Amy. That was the sister I always liked reading about the most.

"There are quite a few other substantial roles in the play as well as these four main ones, and there are also lots of smaller roles." Miss Pritchard paused and smiled around at everyone, and I smiled right back. I was suddenly Cinderella again and she was my fairy godmother – *You shall go to the ball!*

I hung on to her every word because I didn't want to miss a thing or get anything wrong. It would be terrible if I didn't show up at the auditions because I hadn't heard the time right.

"There's a very high standard of acting at Silver Spires, and traditionally this junior play has always been incredibly well received by the parents, which is important because it's a showcase for the school…" She smiled again but then suddenly looked very serious and spoke in a slow, firm voice. "To produce a fine performance I need total commitment from my actors…"

I stood up straight and stuck out my chin. She could rely on *me*, all right. I'd learn all my words overnight and turn up at every rehearsal right on time. I couldn't wait to get started, in fact. *Come on, Miss Pritchard, tell us when the auditions are…*

"So bear that in mind if you're thinking of auditioning for a part. It's great fun being involved in a theater production but it's also hard work and there are sacrifices to be made, such as missing your favorite clubs sometimes, missing television to learn your lines…"

I didn't care. I'd miss every meal as well, if she wanted me to, even though the meals at Silver Spires are mouth-wateringly yum-worthy and eating is one of my favorite activities in the whole world.

"If you'd like to audition for a part you'll need to come to the senior hall, which, for sixth grade students who don't do drama club, is upstairs and along the main corridor in this building..."

She pointed to the ceiling, and I thought back to my first day at Silver Spires when I'd gone exploring for anything to do with drama, and first come across the senior hall and also seen the incredible new theater, which looked like something out of Broadway in New York. It would be so fantastic to perform on that stage.

"I'm going to be doing auditions for eighth graders during their drama lessons on Thursday, and for sixth and seventh graders after school on Thursday, which gives you a few days to prepare yourselves. I've run off copies of mini-scripts and they're on my desk in my office, which is next to the hall. You can help yourselves to those. Choose a speech by the character you want to audition for, but also come armed with an idea of another role you might be interested in, because, of course, you're not necessarily going to be lucky enough to get the first part you want."

Miss Pritchard sat down and Ms. Carmichael

nodded at the music teacher, who pressed play on the CD, and the next minute the hall was filled with some beautiful violin music, or was it cello? Who cared? I just wanted to push past everyone filing out neatly row by row, get a hold of a script and take it to the dorm, then spend the whole day flopped on my bed learning every single word of every single part.

"Bet *you're* happy!" said Mia, tucking her arm through mine when we finally got out of the hall.

"You are *so* right! I am in fact the happiest girl on the planet!" I gabbled as I pulled away and rushed upstairs, taking two steps at a time.

Grabbing a script from the desk in Miss Pritchard's office, I started reading it immediately so I had to walk very slowly to make sure I didn't fall or walk into anyone as I went back downstairs to my friends.

Mia put her arm around me as we left the main building and Grace patted me on the back. "Smooth moves, Georgie! I've never seen you go upstairs so fast!"

Katy laughed. "And look! She's actually concentrating on something. This must be serious!"

"Yes, and it's not easy concentrating with everyone talking!" I said, throwing her an annoyed look, which I quickly turned into a grin because how could I feel annoyed when every single nerve and tendon and sinew and all those other scientific parts of the human body that have always been a mystery to me were glowing brightly and lighting up my life? "I'm going for the part of Amy!" I announced in a voice that came out squeaky with excitement.

It felt so great to hear those words hanging in the air after I'd spoken them that I repeated the main one three times. "Amy, Amy, Amy!" Which made everyone giggle. But then Naomi gently reminded us that hanging around waiting for me to collect the script had made us late for science and we ought to get a move on. So we put on a little spurt and caught up with a group of seventh grade girls just ahead. I was still at the back though, walking slowly so I could read the script at the same time.

"I've never read *Little Women*," I heard Jess say. Then she called back to me, "What's it about? Who's Amy?"

My mind went straight back to the time when I was nine and I got the book in my Christmas stocking. I hadn't wanted to read it at first because it looked so old-fashioned, but Mom had actually sat me down and read the first chapter out loud, and after that I'd been hooked. I remember how I used to keep turning to the front cover to take another look at the picture of the sisters, and even now I can visualize Amy, clear as anything. She had blonde hair that curled at the bottom, blue eyes and a mischievous kind of smile, a little like my younger sister, Roxanne. My hair is a sort of medium brown color and it's just long enough to put in a ponytail without having any short pieces hanging out. It's pretty thick. I used to wish it wasn't, but actually, now I think about it, Amy's hair looks pretty thick. If only I was blonde, that would be even better.

I sighed a happy sigh and caught up with the others. "She's the youngest of the four March sisters and she's bright and bubbly..."

"Like *you*, Georgie!" laughed Naomi. "Typecasting! Terrific!"

"And she's also very artistic, which I know *isn't* like me," I quickly pointed out. "But that's what acting's all about." Then I suddenly realized there was something I hadn't found out. "Are any of you guys going to audition?"

They all started gabbling away at once so I couldn't make out what any of them was saying, but I got the general idea that nobody was that big on the thought of acting.

"I wonder if the students can help paint the sets and scenery for the stage," said Jess, looking thoughtful.

Katy fell into step beside her. "I think I'll find out who's in charge of costumes. I'd love to be—"

One of the seventh grade girls we were passing flung a very haughty look in our direction and interrupted Katy in a know-it-all voice. "Mrs. Chambers is in charge of the wardrobe department, actually, but she won't let you help. She only lets eighth graders."

Katy looked disappointed and Naomi obviously felt sorry for her. "You can always ask, anyway, Kates," she said quietly. "But we'd better go now or we'll be late…"

"See you back at Hazeldean, you two," Mia called over her shoulder as she and Grace went jogging off to their lab with Naomi and Katy, because the four of them all have science together.

Jess and I kept walking with the seventh graders and I wished I had the guts to turn to the know-it-all girl and say, "Did you write the book of life or something?" But sixth graders don't talk to seventh graders like that. You just don't.

"Do the students get to help with the set?" Jess asked her.

The girl shrugged and the expression on her face said she couldn't care less about such a trivial little thing. "You'll have to check with the art department. I'm an actor."

Jess said, "Right," then stopped walking as she seemed to suddenly remember something. "Oh no!" she said. "I've totally forgotten my science textbook – I'll have to run back and get it. Save me a place, Georgie, okay?" And off she went.

As soon as she'd gone, *Miss know-it-all* nodded at the script I was clutching. "So what part are you going for?"

"Amy."

"Amy!" She did a little snort of laughter as though I'd announced that I intended to be the director or something.

Then all her friends started smirking. One of them turned to the know-it-all girl and said, "Wooo, competition for you, Cara," in a sarcastic tone of voice, which made everyone burst into laughter. And another girl rolled her eyes and said, "As if!" which really made my hackles rise.

"What's so funny?" I asked.

"Sorry," said Cara, shaking her head slowly. "I shouldn't laugh really because you wouldn't know, being a sixth grader…"

I didn't like the way she flashed her eyes around all the time she was talking, like she was checking that everyone was still looking at her.

"Know *what*?"

"Well..." She sighed, and spoke really slowly as though all sixth graders were preschoolers. "I mean...you did realize that Amy is one of the four main roles, didn't you? Sorry, what's your name?"

"Georgie." Then I was suddenly sick of being patronized. "Course I realized. I'm not stupid. Anyway, are *you* going to audition?"

She exchanged a look with one of her friends and it was the friend who answered. "Obviously. She's the best actress in Silver Spires. She had a main part in last year's play even though she was only a sixth grader, you know. And that *never* happens."

"So, what part are you going for?" I asked casually.

She reached into her pocket and I wondered for a second whether she'd written it down for some unknown reason, but then she pulled out a little tin, undid it and smeared lipgloss onto her lips. At that moment she just seemed to love herself so much that I really hated her, even though I hardly knew her. It wasn't till she'd put the tin back and rubbed her lips together that she finally deigned to look at me. "Amy," came the answer. She smiled mockingly and my heart sank, but then I tried to give myself a pep talk. Just because everyone thought Cara was a really good actress, it didn't mean that she'd automatically get the part of Amy, did it?

To find out what happens next, read

Ann Bryant's School Days

Who was your favorite teacher?

I had two. Mr. Perks – or Perksy as we called him – because when I was only eleven, he let me work on a play I was writing during class! When I was older, my favorite teacher was Mrs. Rowe, simply because I loved her subject (French) and she was so young and pretty and slim and chic and it was great seeing what new clothes she'd be wearing.

What were your best and worst classes?

My brain doesn't process history, geography or science and I hated cooking, so those were my least favorite subjects. But I was good at English, music, French and PE, so I loved those. I also enjoyed art, although I wasn't very good at it!

What was your school uniform like?

We had to wear a white shirt with a navy blue tie and sweater, and a navy skirt, but there was actually a wide variety of styles allowed – I was a very small person and liked pencil-thin skirts. We all rolled them over and over at the waist!

Did you take part in after-school activities?
Well I loved just hanging out with my friends, but most of all I loved ballet and went to extra classes after school.

Did you have any pets while you were at school?
My parents weren't animal lovers so we were only allowed a goldfish! But since I had my two daughters, we've had loads – two cats, two guinea pigs, two rabbits, two hamsters and two goldfish.

What was your most embarrassing moment?
When I was eleven I had to play piano for assembly. It was April Fool's Day and the piano wouldn't work (it turned out that someone had put a book in the back). I couldn't bring myself to stand up and investigate because that would draw attention to me, so I sat there with my hands on the keys wishing to die, until a teacher came and rescued me!

To find out more about Ann Bryant visit her website: www.annbryant.co.uk